ALSO BY IRENE HANDL

The Sioux

THE
GOLD TIP
PFITZER

THE
GOLD TIP
PFITZER

Irene Handl

1 9 8 6

Alfred A. Knopf *New York*

THIS IS A BORZOI BOOK
PUBLISHED BY ALFRED A. KNOPF, INC.

LIBRARY OF CONGRESS CATALOGING-IN-PUBLICATION DATA

Handl, Irene.
  The Gold Tip Pfitzer.

  I. Title.
PR6058.A564G6   1986   823'.914   85-45593
ISBN 0-394-55088-9

Manufactured in the United States of America

FIRST AMERICAN EDITION

For
NOËL COWARD

Contents

Characters
in The Gold Tip Pfitzer

THE SIOUX

'A.M.X.' Armand-Marie Xavier Benoir, head of the
family. Also known as 'Herman', 'Hermie' and
'Nap'

Marie Benoir, his wife and cousin

Bienville ('Viv') Benoir, his son

Marguerite Castleton née Benoir, his sister

Baudouin Benoir, 'the Skeleton', his younger
brother

Georges-Marie Benoir, Marguerite's son and only
child by her marriage at sixteen to her cousin
Georges. Variously known as 'puss', 'Marie',
'moumou' and 'the Dauphin'

Elaine Benoir, née de Grenier, Bienville's wife

THE CASTLETONS

Vincent Castleton, Marguerite's husband and stepfather to 'the Dauphin'

Cecil Castleton, Castleton's older and favourite
brother

Sybil Castleton, Cecil's wife

Pam and Penny Castleton, older half of Cecil and
 Syb's family
'The Littles' (Samantha, Lydia and Robin),
 younger half

SIOUX STAFF (REMEMBERED FROM 'THE SIOUX')

Madeleine (Mammy), the Dauphin's coloured
 nurse and Armand's childhood mistress
Gustave, butler at the 'Ritz'
Eugène Deckers, the Dauphin's private eye
Marcel Bouzy, the Dauphin's driver
Nicole, Marguerite's maid
Maurice, Marguerite's driver
Colonel and Mme Yves de Chassevent, the
 Dauphin's godparents
Liane de Chassevent is Armand's current mistress

BODS AT THE CLINIQUE BENOIR

Keith Crombie ('Mr Wonderful'), Australian
 children's specialist
Prof. Fabien Courvoisier
Dr Meyer
Dr Frieda Boss-Hart
Directors Dietrich Dieter-Zultz and Walter
 Winkler
Frl Rene Kraus

THE
GOLD TIP
PFITZER

1

Tara the French

Beyond the quaking rim of mud and grass where they are standing, the spumy falls are falling.

Below them there are more, the grovelling cascades almost prostrate in the grass like greybeards quarrelling.

They are in the Jura. They are in the Vosges. Castleton hasn't the faintest idea where they are. It's only two days since they left Paris but they seem to have been travelling ever since the boy's funeral three weeks ago.

Above them they can see Castleton's brother-in-law. Armand Benoir, standing sentinel beside the two cars, coat collar turned up against the waterchilled air, awaiting the final decision.

Above him, the slow-moving traffic of the skies, each cloud waiting patiently behind the other before lumbering on, while on the motorway below the cars rave past. Perhaps towards Paris.

'What are we supposed to be looking at?' Marguerite wants to know.

Castleton has no idea.

She turns on her heel. He follows her up the steep

track, the sound of quarrelling waters receding as they climb.

Mim in her knickerbocker suit. Feet flicking upwards in kicky schoolboy boots.

He hates this whole new presentation of herself. Clever, ill-humoured, and designed expressly to seal the epoch for them both.

Before they reach the top he manages to get in: 'I suppose you'll marry that sod Perrerez directly the divorce comes through?'

She shrugs a non-denial.

Perrerez, the frigging frigorifico from the Argentine, who was chasing Mim when Castleton first met her, through her brother in Paris. Castleton shouts after her: 'I hope he serves you right!'

She must have heard because she's waiting for him as he rounds a rock.

'What did you say?'

'You heard.'

She swings out at him with her shoulder-bag. 'Take that from me then!'

He aims a swipe at her behind, but misses. She's already capering off to her Benoir. She's such a bitch she makes him want to laugh.

And all the while the milky seeds of thistles are following them up the track in ever-turning undulating chains.

A few sprint delicately past, while thousands more pour down on them from the top of the bank where rank upon rank are growing in August pride amongst the tyre tracks around the two parked cars.

He gains the top as she is having her bootlace tied for her by her brother. He seems to have accepted the whole whisky-swigging, Gauloise-smoking disguise. That sent-up haircut. Her near-denial that she has ever had a child.

He remarks, smiling: 'Put your gloves on, Mi. It's cold, their Switzerland, you know.'

So that is where they are.

Nobody says anything after that so Benoir helps his sister into the Rolls. This seems to be the end of the relationship; pointless to press negotiations further.

There is an invisible mark in the road. A kind of neutral zone. Benoir steps into it.

'What will you do now, Vince?'

Transfer to Hong Kong or Tokyo. Preferably Tokyo. He hasn't yet decided.

'But first you'll go to London?'

Lord, yes. Since they're in Switzerland, he means to make the four o'clock plane from Zurich.

'Perfect. I'll call you at your brother's then, tonight.'

'Righto.'

An electrically operated window whirrs down in the Rolls. Marguerite calls out in French: 'Are you coming, Armand, or what?'

Since the kid's death she has affected a new way of talking. A particularly insufferable brand of that daft 'Boul' Mich' the whole of fashionable Paris seems currently to be talking.

The window whirrs smartly up again. Benoir steps back into the combat zone.

'Jusqu'à ce soir, alors.'

' 'Bye.' Castleton sees his brother-in-law's small hand wave once before the car shoots forward and down through the planted fir forest to meet the motorway below. So that's the end of the two days' truce. Not a flicker from Herself, of course. From the already-as-good-as ex-Mrs Castleton. She really is an artist at it, old Mim, he has to give her that. He decides to be glad about it. It's probably the last he'll see of either of them, anyway. Unless he decides to defend when their case comes up in the Paris courts. It's quite a thought. It might be worth it just to see Benoir's face when he sees what has blown in from across the Channel to spill the marital haricots.

Castleton grins. Benoir the Great Arranger. It would be fun to gum up all his clever plans for sparing his sacred sister's feelings.

A momentary regret goes through him as he thinks how very much he had liked Benoir throughout their association. He will again. If things ever get back to normal. As he feels now he wouldn't even wish the boy alive again. Too much of a drag. Tara. Tara the French. He walks over to the Bentley, the thistles still pressing on his heels, still filing importantly past on milky feet.

There is even one on the driving seat, rocking and rolling gently from side to side. Let it stay. The Sioux have got each other. He'll have this Swiss chap for a travelling companion.

The Sioux are the Benoirs who call themselves The Sioux because of their fierce tribalism which causes their fierce tickers to beat as one. The Sioux are indivisible. But he is driving back to his people as one gets back into a car after a crash. Or never, never drives again.

2

Moumou Canaille

Hands stuck in pockets, knees up to her chin, squatting like an Arab in the passenger seat cadging a light.

'Du feu du feu du feu,' chants Marguerite. Her brother lights her cigarette from his, but when she tries to snatch his hand he promptly puts it back on the wheel.

'I'm driving, Mi,' points out Benoir. He's very angry with her.

She recognized all the signs of what she and her brother Baudouin secretly call 'la formule A.-M.X.' after his given names.

Lowered lashes. Delicate level frown. Fastidious profile averted from 'the culprit'. Later, her nephew Bienville had been let into the club.

Her sweet Armand-Marie Xavier, how she adores him. 'Espèce d'idiot,' grumbles Marguerite eyeing him fondly from under the loaded visor of her preposterous cap and goggles.

'What are you cross about, you fool? Why are you making your shit-face at me?'

She is quite astonished when Benoir takes the car off

the road and runs it on to the verge. 'But what is happening? Benoir! Are you out of your mind?'

He has actually switched the engine off under some sort of terrible Swiss tree. She is so furious she pummels him with her fists but he just tells her coldly: 'Stop it, Mi.'

My God. This time it really looks as if she's going to catch it! She complains loudly: 'Ah non, Armand, tu sais! It isn't fair!'

She knows she has behaved badly, but all the same for once he must agree she has had provocation. She's rubbing her face against his collar which holds the scent she loves best in all the world. On top of this she has just discovered that the seal-fur is delicious to taste with the tip of her tongue. She nibbles it warily, with one eye cocked on her brother. He is the dearest, most beautiful person on earth and she wants very much not to be scolded by him.

No use. He's going to scold her. To save her neck she calls out quickly, 'Oh, look! A Schwiss *jam*-tree!' She has just noticed the tree they are under is a cherry, and is now insisting loudly that in the correct season the cherry trees of Switzerland are loaded, not with fruit, but with neat half-kilo pots of good Swiss cherry jam.

'Aoh, I shay, *Almond*!' Marguerite says in her special 'Castleton' voice. 'What a *schream*! Aoh, I *shay*, Almond!' calls Marguerite, who is batting both eyes very fast while keeping them skinned for signs of a possible crack-up. Nothing. Pointless to run it any further. That bougre isn't even smiling. Marguerite thinks: he still doesn't like it when I take Vincent off.

Well, it wasn't very funny, anyway, but moumou would have loved it.

'Where are you going, Marguerite?'

She is going to stretch her legs. Since he seems to have made up his mind they are going to be stuck on top of this bank for ever. She is almost out of the car when he takes her by the arm.

'Stay where you are.'

What for? She wants to make pipi. She's even jigging about on the seat. 'If I wet my pants it will be your fault, you pig.' My God! The way that prude is staring at her one might think she was already doing it!

'For once in your life try to behave like a normal being.' He is utterly and completely disgusted with her. Has he stopped the car just to tell her that? She's hungry and wants her lunch.

'What did you say?'

She doesn't quite dare repeat it. Instead she grumbles: 'What are you shouting at me for? It's not my fault the marriage crashed.'

On the contrary. It is entirely her fault. Given time, Vincent would have probably been willing to restart the association. Which was the whole object of their coming here.

She defends herself hotly. It's not true! Benoir is always accusing her of being unhelpful, but she had given Castleton every chance to get over the shock of moumou's death. Three weeks should have been more than sufficient for any man who wasn't also imagining himself to be the father, but it seems Castleton had been either unable or unwilling to make the effort, so she had taken the rational decision for them both.

She bursts out: 'Oh, let's get out of this horrible country with their yodelling cows!' She has no idea why

any of them had come here in the first place. 'Everyone's hash could have been settled twice as quickly in
Paris. Without cows,' adds Marguerite. In any case there
had never been any serious idea of restarting the marriage.
At least, not on her part. What was in Castleton's mind
she doesn't know.

'Or care.'

What would be the use of caring? She knows that even
now she has only to lift a finger for Castleton to grasp
it with both hands. But she refuses to be drawn. It would
only lead to more and more talks. Further discussions
about their future which would all lead inevitably to the
past. To her son. To moumou. Moumou canaille. She
is disconsolate. He is disconsolate. They are both disconsolate. And the sum of their desolations is inconceiv-
able boredom.

That kind of half-life would be valueless for them both.

She states quite calmly: 'It isn't possible to go on
being bored for ever.'

'I see.'

She points out snidely: 'In any case no one will press
him for alimony, so what are you fussing about?' It's
the kind of *vulgaire* remark that Benoir detests most, so
she's not surprised at getting no reply. He's even smiling,
but she is not deceived. She has learnt by now that
Benoir's smile is not reliable evidence of what he is
actually thinking.

He looks at her briefly and then starts the car.

'Where are we going?' asks Marguerite.

The Rolls backs silently down the bank on to the road
again.

'Benoir!'

'What?'

For the second time of asking, where are they going?

Home. They are going to lunch at Montreux, and then they are going home.

Marguerite protests instantly: 'Ah non, tu sais!' It will be too boring if they go back to Paris straight away after lunch. Marie will still be in bed and, anyway, the house is like a morgue these days.

'Let's go to Italy.' They can overnight at the Bolzano-Castel and dance. Marguerite coaxes: 'You can ring Zurich from Montreux. Tell them to throw a few things in a bag and take the next flight out. I shall only need Nicole. And my small jewel case, tell her. They can take the big pieces back to Paris when Maurice runs the other car home tonight.' She promises there will be no difficulty about reservations. Since their honeymoon, the Castel has always kept a suite for Georges and herself.

She thinks, My God, Georges has already been dead for nearly five years. And now this other one has run away from her as well!

She remembers Georges' excitement at the birth of his son. ' 'Garde moi ton copain, veux tu, Mi? Il a des petites ongles, et tout, et tout. Il est formidable, celui-là!'

It will really do her good to get away from the whole mess for a few days.

Marguerite urges: 'Be sweet. Do it for me, Benoir.'

Nothing could be further from his intentions than to please her. 'I have wasted enough time as it is.'

Then will he tell her what they have been doing stopping in the middle of nowhere for hours? 'And hours and hours?' says Marguerite.

Because for an instant he had thought she could be

made to see how disgustingly she had behaved and the
extent of the damage caused by her attitude. 'I was mis-
taken, of course.'

'Of course.' She isn't even listening. She's busy trying
to make him change his mind about going back to Paris.
'We will be back a few hours later than originally intended, voilà tout.' If he is worried about Marie he
needn't be. Whatever time they arrive his wife will still be
in her bed!

It was the wrong thing to say. Benoir says curtly: 'Non,
j'ai dit non. Terminé.'

She has lost – and through her own stupidity. Now
nothing can save her from being taken straight home after
lunch. 'Ah, merde!' cries Marguerite.

She has grabbed his handkerchief and is blowing her
nose and swearing. 'Merde! Merde! Merde!'

Her brother advises her cheerfully: 'Don't cry, tough-
guy. Tears are for ladies. I refuse to be seduced.' Incidentally, if she still wants to go somewhere she'd better
hurry up. He intends to hit the Nationale 9 for Paris
not a second later than two o'clock.

She says in a choked voice: 'If I'm such a horrible
character, why d'you still bother with me?'

He answers, smiling: 'You're a bad habit I got into
years ago, why should I drop you now?'

'Smug prig.' She wriggles down from the car without
his proffered assistance and makes off along the verge,
kicking at flints.

Her brother shouts after her: 'Hey, you! Want me to
keep watch?'

After his last remark, definitely not. She wants only
loyal persons around her.

He bursts out laughing. 'Big deal! I suppose you think the whole world is competing for the honour of seeing your ass!'

'Ass yourself!' calls Marguerite. He's coming after her but she pretends not to see. She's busy admiring her boots kicking up stones. She loves her kicky, tough-guy boots. She wants Benoir to love them, too. But he does not. He has already made it plain that he likes very little about her at the present moment. Certainly not her boots which he has accused of being part of an outfit expressly devised by her to precipitate the end of her marriage.

It's not true! She attacks him with lumps of earth and grass roots from a foxhole of a ditch. It simply isn't true that she has ever deliberately dressed in a way to alienate her husband!

It's true and she knows it. That drag is a piece of sheer bad manners. Anyone else would have tried at least to soften the blow. But she has behaved with a brutality which disgusts him beyond words.

All the same, he seems to have scraped enough of them together to lecture her with. She mutters sulkily: 'I thought they would amuse you, my bags.'

On a girl of sixteen, perhaps. On a woman of twenty-seven, not at all. In any case it doesn't matter any more. 'You've crashed everyone's lives for them as usual. I hope you're satisfied.' What is interesting him at the moment is where she intends to do her business. Not in full view of the road, he hopes. 'There are adequate bushes over there, Marguerite.'

She isn't looking for bushes. She refuses to sit on a thistle just to please him. She doesn't care who sees her, and if he doesn't stop lecturing she will squat down on this very spot and give that prude of a Benoir a heart attack. She hopes all the cars in Switzerland go flashing by. Especially the Bentley. It would be terribly funny if, just as the Bentley was passing, she turned herself to the road so that the last glimpse ever Castleton caught of his darling wife was her bare bottom!

She's falling about at the idea, but Benoir has caught her by the slack of her pants and is bumrushing her towards the bushes. 'Petite sans gêne. Tu n'as pas de honte?' But he is laughing as well.

Oh, Benoir, her darling brother. If he should ever stop loving her, how could she go on living? How would she even exist?

'Hurry up, Mi! What are you doing behind there?'

She gives him two guesses. Oh, this is like old times again. Going for walks as children at St Eze, Armand would scandalize the governesses by keeping watch for her and Beau.

'Dis donc! You make a noise like a she-camel when you piss!'

She shoots out of the bushes, her teeth chattering with cold. Quickly, back to the car and put the heater on! Her bum, her face, her hands and feet are all like ice! Back, back to the car! Let them throw their damn Alps to the cows.

They race back, whooping and pelting each other with ripped-out bracken and grass.

'Quickly, get in, Mi! What are you waiting for?'

She's waiting for a kiss. He kisses her. She keeps on asking for another. 'One more. One more for the road.' He gives her a last kiss and bundles her into the car. His coat is round her shoulders. Her hands are in his gloves. She's almost convinced he loves her as much as ever.

She says in a satisfied voice : 'I think you would always love me, whatever I did.'

'Don't bank on it,' advises her brother. He laps the car robe round her legs. 'Now shut up, Mi, and let me drive in peace.'

She lets him drive till they get to the boggy end waters of the lake, where dwarf alders and black birches are growing amongst the sparkling shale. A train like a clock-work toy is burrowing busily in and out of the mountain on the opposite side. They can hear its rattle, loud in the sunlight, silent in the tunnels. Loud and then silent. Then suddenly loud again. Going to Italy.

'Look, Mi.' Her brother is pointing at the lake, where white mists are burning off the white water, and suddenly all the slaty mountains are steepling in the sun. 'It's really charming when the sun shines.'

She doesn't want to look. She wants to go to Italy. Nobody in Paris is expecting them tonight, which means that after dinner they'll be completely marooned unless they take in a late show or a cinema. 'If I know you you'll probably want to telephone your mistress for hours.'

'It's not to be ruled out.'

'Charming for her ! In the meanwhile what am I supposed to be doing ?'

He answers calmly : 'You will be seeing your secretary about your arrangements for going to the Argentine. Even for you a fourth marriage will take a little organizing.' He adds drily : 'From what one hears, it's an extraordinary country, Argentina. You should fit into it extremely well.'

As what he has just said is obviously not intended for a compliment, she has no wish to take it up. Instead she says in a belligerent tone, 'I suppose you also intend to phone that degenerate when you get back to Paris?'

If by degenerate she means his son, most certainly he does.

She bursts out furiously: 'My son hasn't been three weeks in his grave but you have forgiven that creature already.'

He doesn't see the connection. 'Whether I forgive Viv or not will change nothing. It will certainly not bring puss back to you.'

She cuts in: 'He couldn't even bother to be in time to see his cousin. My son died in his blood, but why should he let that disturb his honeymoon?'

'Viv was afraid,' Benoir points out.

'He showed his true face this time, your son whom you have idolized, whom you have made a God of all his life!'

He is frightfully pale.

'You're a weakling, Benoir. A doormat for everyone to wipe his filthy feet on.'

'It's valueless to carry punishment beyond a certain point.'

For him, perhaps. Not for her. She'll hold her spite against Bienville till the day she dies.

That's only because she is an exceptionally nasty person. He tells her quietly: 'You are forgetting that I love my son, Mimi.' He advises her: 'By the way, Mi, you should allow yourself to think of puss from time to time. It will do you good. After all, you have worked like a beaver all these years to keep him from the rest of us. Now

he is wholly yours again you must enjoy him, or it will all
have been a great waste of your time.'

Oh, he is cruel. He can be terribly cruel.

One other thing, Benoir advises her : 'Don't have a
child by this fourth marriage. With a kid there will be
an even bigger mess.' Besides which, she makes a horrible
mother. 'You have a positive talent for it, you know.'

They drive in silence till they are practically in the
suburbs of Montreux. He asks her where she would like
to eat. If she has no preference he suggests Weber's. He
hears they are famous for their trout.

She has no preference and, for his information, she
isn't hungry any more.

He tells her kindly : 'Choose something splendid. Your
appetite will come back as you eat. And Mi. . . .'

'What?'

After Perrerez no more marriages. 'Enough is enough,'
says Benoir.

3

Déménagement International

A little weak sunlight has got trapped in the fork of a tree and is burning like an electric bulb among the lower branches.

She will wait on the terrace till Benoir has finished his telephoning. 'Order for me too, Mi.' He will be with her as soon as he has talked to Marie.

Idiot, don't run, thinks Marguerite, watching the boyish figure disappear into the restaurant. You'll be back soon enough in the nursery with that baby you married.

That permanent invalid. She will be worse than ever now. With moumou's death she has the perfect alibi. By now she has surely persuaded herself that it is she who has lost a son. First Castleton, now Marie. It must be catching.

Marguerite thinks: What a life my brother leads with that half-wit. She's too stupid even to watch television. After mass her maid brings her her jewellery to play with. If she does two consecutive rows of her petit-point it's a record. After lunch she sleeps for two hours until five o'clock. If it's fine she takes goûter somewhere in the Bois

with her equally brainless friends. If it rains they come
to her. At nine o'clock dinner is served and my poor
brother has to listen to everything that has happened
during her entire day. Which is precisely nothing. How
many times Rose has had to run to Foquet's to match the
exact shade of silk for her next tapestry. How often the
butler has had to take that incontinent little brute of a
dog of hers into the garden and the precise stage its
cystitis has now reached. At ten-thirty she drinks her
tisane, and after that, good night! Her day is over, she
disappears to her bed!

A normal man would beat her like a carpet, but
Armand has the patience of a saint with that silly fool.

Marguerite thinks angrily: he has spoiled his whole
life for an idea! He only married her because she
resembles our mother in looks. What a price he has had
to pay for his fantasies ever since!

Even their honeymoon was a fiasco. They were supposed to go round the world, but with that little provincial they only got as far as Rome. She was homesick
for her father and, believe it or not, *for the sisters at her
convent*, the St Esprit!

My God, what my brother must have put up with
during that first year while the child was coming. He
must have been driven half out of his mind with boredom. She was exactly like a child herself. That great
swing Armand had put up for her in the orangerie at
Neuilly. She had liked nothing better than to have him
swing her. Until she became enceinte, after which complete stultification had set in. She had refused to show
herself even at a cinema or virtually to budge from her
room.

Marguerite knows for a fact that the whole household over there is run by the servants. If there's a mess-up it's always Armand who is presented with it, never she.

And what a prude! Benoir had had to teach her everything. He had once confided that when they were first married Marie had even tried to get into her bath in her chemise! It was an open joke between them that Marie had ever got as far as producing a child. And that only because, poor wretched man, he had stayed with her throughout the accouchement.

Lucky for her she had my brother to teach her, thinks Marguerite. He was so gentle he never tried to force her, but of course he soon learned to look elsewhere for his pleasures.

During the early years of his marriage Benoir had changed his mistresses twice a day! But since the birth of his son life with Marie had forced him completely out of character, which, of course, can be the only reason why his affaire with Liane de Chassevent has lasted so long!

She is still probably congratulating herself that she alone has discovered the art of keeping Benoir's affections!

All the same, everyone knows that her brother's alliance with Liane is one of the happiest non-marriages in Paris.

Incidentally, Liane still talks to Marie daily on the telephone, most probably while she and Benoir are actually in bed together. Marie, of course, is fully convinced that Liane is her best friend. Marguerite thinks: Even a child has to grow up. Only my sister-in-law remains the same. If they did the full business in front

of her she would still not believe Benoir had been un-
faithful.

The head waiter has come out on the terrace armed
with the usual outsize bills of fare followed by a waiter
and the sommelier.

'Would Madame care to order now?'

'No, I will wait for Monsieur.' Marguerite thinks: In
case you are hoping to save yourself a second journey.
'Bring me another Scotch on the rocks and get rid of these
billboards.'

They collect the menus and vanish. She smiles when
her drink is put before her. How both men had hated it
when she had started drinking whisky directly after the
death. At first she had forced herself to it in order to
change her image. Now she quite likes it for itself.

Moumou canaille. What things that tramp had forced
her to with his dying! If she had him to hand now she
would slap him till her palm tingled.

Oh, no. She wouldn't. If she could have him back
for only one hour she would go down on her knees and
ask his pardon for her behaviour to him all his short
life.

In any case he's bound to get his revenge now, that
one. The minute he sees his father up there he'll tell him
everything, as usual. It suddenly strikes her that by the
time she sees them again those two will still be young.
Georges was twenty-two when she had lost him, moumou
only nine. And she'll be an old woman. What a charming thought! If she really believed in an after-life she'd
do herself in here and now.

She blows a kiss at her brother who is just coming
out to join her at their table.

That pig, Marguerite thinks, smiling, he looks happier for even those few moments away from me! He is probably delighted that the decisive day has come and definite steps towards the divorce can now be taken. Perhaps as early as next week, even. In France, with money, everything's possible.

Of course he would probably have liked it still better if Castleton and she had remained together. To build their life afresh! She will let him cling to his illusions. For her part she will run like the devil to Perrerez and thank her stars she has her son to herself again.

As to this other child, everyone is always accusing her of being selfish, but she had been perfectly willing to give Castleton his choice as to what is to be done in respect of his son or daughter or whatever it turns out to be. She had asked him outright if he wanted an abortion, it was all the same to her. Only, as she had told him, 'if you want one, make up your mind, because I shan't do it after the end of this month.'

He had stood staring at her as if he were too appalled to speak, so in the end she had left him without getting any answer from him at all.

N'importe. It doesn't matter since she has no intention of keeping the child, whatever it is, boy or girl. She has told Castleton that she will pack it off to him complete with layette and nurse as soon as possible after the birth. She will probably have it by Caesarian and if everything goes as her accoucheur predicts she need lose no more than six weeks over the whole transaction. Everything else can be settled from Paris via Benoir, or direct from Buenos Aires.

Thank God Perrerez has absolutely no feeling for anything except his bull fights and his polo. She will not get a bad press from him as she does from Benoir for refusing to exhibit her feelings about her dead son. With Perrerez she can continue to be the most self-possessed woman in Buenos Aires as long as she is also the most alluring. With him she will be safe at last. Safe from the Great British Sympathy. Free from the sight of her sister-in-law convincing herself a little more each day that she's a hopeless invalid and unable to rally after moumou's death. My God, what vapours. What hot-and-cold compresses in darkened rooms. And on top of it that pack of servants participating in it all.

Which reminds her. She must get rid of her lot before she leaves for the Argentine. A good opportunity to dump the whole rabble on Benoir. His house will be bulging with them, though of course he'll be delighted to get his beloved Mado back. She had been Bienville's nurse before she had been moumou's, and also, something of far more importance to that sentimentalist, she had been Armand's first mistress at home, when they were both fourteen. Well, he can have her back with Marguerite's compliments. One more voice to swell the chorus of hosannas around Marie's bed.

That Benoir. The only amusing thing in this whole sinflood of tears has been watching to see how much of this stuff he will be able to swallow. It has been really funny to see him sacrificing himself for them all as surely as if he had cut his throat from ear to ear.

As he comes up she calls out cheekily: 'Don't tell me you have finished with your telephoning already. I haven't ordered a thing.'

This good news has already been relayed to him by

the maître d'hôtel, so he has made the order for them both.

What if she doesn't like what he has ordered? He assures her, smiling : 'You'll eat it and like it, my girl.'

They study the wine list together. She feels much happier now. She has suddenly made up her mind to have an abortion. If Castleton complains about it, it can't be helped. He should have staked his claim at the beginning when he'd been asked. She will not risk her health or waste her time by waiting one moment longer for anyone.

4

The Semi-Silent Minority

Since then, of course, it has become clear to Castleton that what had been happening was a remission that had lasted a long time.

They have been at St Eze since the middle of May, and his doctors still say they don't want to see the boy till July, when they'll be back in Paris anyway for routine checks. By July also Castleton hopes he will have been able to persuade the Sioux to let a new man take a look at George. The Australian surgeon, Keith Crombie.

Crombie's name had first been put forward by Castleton's brother, Cecil, who'd run across him during this last lot in the Far East. At present he's reported to be working wonders in London with kids in even worse nick than Mim's chap.

It might be possible to fly him over to Paris.

'Bonne idée,' Benoir had told him, smiling.

If he means what he says it's a piece of cake. Old Mim will never knowingly go against a wish of Benoir's once it has been expressed.

Meanwhile they're at St Eze, an ancient manoir in the Auvergne, built on the site of a nunnery supposed to have been founded by a natural daughter of Louis the Good. Inside, what is not Louis Seize is Louis Treize, but the Sioux like it that way.

It seems they originally came from this part of Central France and St Eze had been a favourite country seat of Mim's old man. She and her brothers had spent most of their childhood here.

Now a heat wave has driven them all into the garden and is keeping them there from breakfast until late after dinner at night. No rain has fallen for a fortnight. They might be in Africa the heat is so intense. The nightingales sing all day and the Dauphin has worked up an alarming appetite and is now never seen without something to eat in his hand. A brioche, a pear, a saucer of tiny fried fish to eat in his fingers.

Everyone else at St Eze is tremendously bucked about this except Castleton, who doesn't know how to vote. He has become the semi-silent minority.

He cheers himself up with the thought that the Dauphin isn't as pale here as he is in Paris. At least, in the shade he's not.

In the sun he turns a blinding white and a kind of snow-light obliterates his features.

'Come out of the sun, ducky,' Castleton says.

He comes into the shade and climbs on to Castleton's knee. He's still a pretty turnip-lantern with moony cheeks. But it's all right. He's got features.

'Are you well, my darling?' enquires the Dauphin solicitously. He is devouring a lark and his dark glasses give him the look of an owlet. A tiny leg with claw protrudes from his jaws.

'C'est bon, ça, vous savez,' remarks the Dauphin pushing the rest of the bird into Castleton's mouth.

'Look out. You're giving it all to me.'

'Keep it.' The Dauphin says firmly: 'I can get some more.' He shares the Sioux enthusiasm for finger-feeding anyone he likes. They all do it. Even that bloody pet monkey of his brother-in-law's, Ouistiti, never stops cramming rubbish into everyone's mouth.

'Ought he to eat so much, darling?' Castleton asks. He's been watching his stepson bunking along to the kitchens through the midday glare, his arms wrapped tightly in the arms of Marcel Bouzy, his chauffeur, and Eugène Deckers, his detective.

He's been using this kind of support for a couple of weeks now.

Castleton points out: 'It's almost lunch time, darling.'

Marguerite shrugs. 'If he doesn't eat, that doesn't please you either.'

Deckers goes everywhere with him here. The vast forests that surround St Eze make it a high-risk kidnap area. Depressing.

'He'll spoil his appetite for lunch,' says Castleton, the semi-silent minority.

'Moumou!'

He turns round at the sound of her voice. His magic face with the dissolving features is turning blank again.

'Walk properly.' Marguerite calls out: 'You two! What're you thinking of? You are letting him waltz about like a cripple!'

They wait for further instructions, but that's the whole

message. Because it was he who brought it up, not one single dicky about not eating between meals!

They start to move off again at a more cautious pace. It's amazing to watch the patience of the men.

Like Benoir, the Dauphin is tremendously popular with the servants.

'Which is more than you are, moosh,' says Castleton.

'Comment?'

'Popular.'

'With whom?'

'With anybody.'

'Et puis?'

'That's all,' says Castleton, kissing her. 'You're absolutely lovely.'

But she's not listening. She must have heard Benoir arrive because, without a word, she jumps up suddenly and leaves him.

That's me sorted out then, thinks Castleton, grinning. Sounds of conviviality from the kitchens proclaim the Dauphin is being given a standing ovation while chefs and master chefs vie with each other to tempt this splendid brand-new appetite that everyone is voting for except Castleton.

The Dauphin's two favourites are Sylvestre, chef patissier, and Nicéphore, maître chef and native of Auvergne.

He stands between their short, stout legs, their portly thighs, doing himself no good at all banging away with a teaspoon at their bloody cuisine classique de France, la plus soignée du monde, while all around him the lower echelons pluck, mince, chop and marinate in preparation for the great nightly spree of dinner.

Alone, under his shady tree, Castleton lights a cigar. It's terrifically hot in here among the spires and umbels of expiring weeds and the hot dinnery smells of peppermint and wild garlic.

The birds are silent. Only an occasional insect pings past and cockchafers, themselves like flying walnuts, whirr doggedly on towards the walnut groves.

It's been an early spring, and already the industrious chafers have nearly stripped the trees.

Someone is practising the piano in the salon. Nobody else plays, so it must be Mim. There is no further evidence of Benoir's arrival. Castleton starts to grin. She just up and left him to get shot of him. It's as simple as that.

Depressing, but funny with it. St Eze stands basking on top of its tapestry hill, among its tapestry groves and vineyards. Oak forest extends as far as eye can see, a heavy carpet flung over a landscape of dead volcanoes and ruined chapels.

This is the cradle of the wicked Sioux. Werewolves are said to flunk around these woods, and the grounds contain a holy well reputed to work miracles.

The Sioux are very serious-minded about miracles, while availing themselves of the latest achievements of modern science, and Castleton wouldn't be a bit surprised if the sacred fountain of Eze wasn't their chief reason for lugging the kid all the way down here for seven weeks. Vipers drink from the overflow, issuing from the woods at dawn before the mists have cleared.

Vipers drink only from the purest source. The Dauphin, who is enjoying a religious turn-on, assures him in a hollow voice, 'It's on account of the cross on their backs.'

He, himself, takes the water twice a day from his

cupped hands. It's not a done thing to use a glass. 'Except it is a holy vessel,' amends the Dauphin meaningfully.

Servants are set to diligently collect the delicate maidenhair fern that trembles in the cold, still air round the lip of the holy well. From this is made a famous sirop de capillaire esteemed by the Sioux as a sovereign cure for 'anaemias of every type' and for the 'purification of the principal organs'.

There is also an ink-like Avernat, a dreadful plonk specially grown for the Dauphin's benefit on the most craggy and hostile of the home-slopes of St Eze itself.

This monstrous tipple is tipped to buck him up, calm him down, and never mind about leaving him drunk for most of the day.

Luckily, the Dauphin is quite agreeable to having miracles worked on him, and having nostrums pumped into him by his family and friends.

He loves everything about St Eze, especially the were-wolves. He, personally, has spoken with a forestier who has shot at the hindquarters of a loup-garou as it trotted off through the bushes crying like a woman, and he will gorge himself upon the cèpes which grow in the many scores of cercles de fées at the exact point where the miraculous water re-enters the ground to be seen no more by mortal eye.

Well, hooray for the Dauphin whose woods are still stuffed with unicorns and gryphons.

He notices that the piano has suddenly stopped. There is a second's silence then Mim comes pelting out of the house.

What ho, Benoir, thinks Castleton. He steps over

flattened and expiring weeds out of his grotto into the day where fortress-high clouds are building up.

'Hullo, Benoir,' calls Castleton.

They greet each other warmly, 'Alors, mon vieux, ça marche?' As usual with Benoir, the carry-on is beyond belief. He has brought his entire entourage down from Paris for the weekend.

His wife, his mistress, and Liane's husband, that model of soldierly probity, Colonel de Chassevent.

'Ah non, Armand,' protests Marguerite. 'What a bore!' Her brother says simply: 'Don't worry, we'll think of something. He wanted to see puss.'

Yves de Chassevent is George's godfather.

'We will divide him between us,' promises Benoir. He is turning his attention to a second Rolls which his great friend and secretary, Jean-Luc Schreiber, has ferried down with all the Benoir paraphernalia of valet, maids, luggage and a minute ailing Japanese spaniel belonging to Marie Benoir.

'Here, take your child! The news is good, she slept the whole way. Jean-Luc reports no sickness.' His own pet monkey, the delinquent Ouistiti, is riding on his shoulder.

The little blighter is making faces at everyone. With his pug face, and in light chains connecting low-slung belt to jewelled collar, he looks, at least to Castleton's eyes, more of a malefactor than ever. The Dauphin, stoned as usual, is in ecstacies.

Everyone is being counted amid gales of laughter. Everyone is there, and everyone is pleased to see Castleton except Mim and Ouistiti, who are no hypocrites.

The Dauphin, on the other hand, is extremely pleased

to see him and insists on shaking hands with him à l'anglaise.

He is greeting everybody and being soundly kissed on both cheeks in return. He is clutching a blood-stained pear. Everything he puts his teeth into is streaked with blood, but nobody remarks upon it any more.

When Castleton had first noticed he had panicked, but kind Benoir had explained that this type of bleeding was unimportant as it came from the gums, and after that the subject had been closed for serious discussion.

Jokes are quite in order, of course. Jokes are encouraged.

Benoir calls out gaily: 'What d'you think of little Benoir's appetite, Vince?'

'I think it's bloody marvellous,' answers Castleton neatly and wins himself a laugh.

It's nice not being a minority any more. He likes not being the Grouch of St Eze. The Sioux are absolutely right. They know what's what. They have things in perspective and keep them there.

'Let's go in, Vincent,' urges Marguerite, who appears to be speaking to him again. 'We shall all get sun-stroke in this heat.'

Besides, she is sick of eating in the garden. She has ordered lunch indoors, and she has put her arm through Castleton's.

Now he has recognized the Dauphin's appetite he's going to vote for it like everybody else. He'll join the majority. Then he'll be happy about everything except Mim.

What she's just given him is useless. Not at all up to snuff.

The evil-doing Ouistiti is whistling like a bird while baring his teeth at Castleton like a dog.

At the same time he's moving his scalp up and down at a terrific speed and masturbating with both his small, black-gloved hands at such a rate he nearly falls off Benoir's shoulder.

'Alors, c'est déjà terminé ou quoi?' demands Benoir. But he is laughing all the same.

'O, Ouisti, you bad thing!' exclaims the Dauphin, entranced. It's too hot to play now, but later on when it is cooler, he's looking forward to mafficking with his rompish and disorderly friend.

A few drops of rain have already fallen and are scattering the party left and right. They are all racing for the house with newspapers and the men's coats over their heads in a laughing, disorganized crowd. It's a rout.

Only the colonel, left in command, is treating the thing as a military exercise. He brings up the rear in a disciplined fashion, and conducts his godson to a prepared position out of the path of the attacking storm.

At the house a magnificent luncheon is waiting to be served in the great flagged salle à manger, where vast oak logs, whole tree trunks from the Forest of Eze are already flaming and hissing behind the glass chimney screen and all is Henri IV and lovely grub.

Outside the window the dog-day has turned a pasty white. The splash of the spring in the grounds is very marked and loud.

Nothing is happening yet. Only laconic sheets of lightning show up the deep-slit eyes and nostrils, the Saracen features of the back face of St Eze.

The front face remains smiling at a still light blue

patch of sky, at the little jewelled gardens that emerge from forest lawns of brightest green.

For an instant both faces of the house are brilliantly lit up in strong relief, then both go out as rain obliterates everything and the clouds move in to drop their fire bombs.

On valleys, forests, crags, a rain of fire falls on everything, except the two-faced Janus-house whose grounds contain the sacred spring of Eze.

5

The Artificial Date

One morning, about a week before his death, the Dauphin, Georges-Marie Benoir, forgot all his English. Totally and tracelessly, as if he had never known any language but French.

He has come back from his morning drive in the park with Marcel and Deckers virtually speechless in so far as his English is concerned.

'My God, moumou,' exclaims his mother.

'Never mind, darling, it'll come back,' says Castleton, kissing her.

He seems fairly hopeless at lunch, but Castleton's not worried. He's got everything crossed for August One when Crombie flies over to take a look at him. He's got his brother Cecil to thank for that. He'd gone to no end of trouble to get this Aussie out to Paris in return for something old Cecil had been able to do for him when they both were stationed at Singapore during the war.

From what Cecil tells him, Crombie's considered pretty

35

much on a par with the Benoirs' man Courvoisier in the study of leukaemia and diseases of the blood.

One's a surgeon, the other primarily a medical man. You pays yer money and yer takes yer choice. Ideally, Castleton is hoping for a coalition.

Considering they none of 'em want him, the Sioux have been pretty good about Crombie. Mim hasn't uttered (while thinking plenty) and Benoir has booked him in at the Bristol. Actually, he'd have preferred to put Crombie up at the Ritz as the Sioux call their place at Neuilly, but the Sioux are a bit weird about asking people into their homes. Marie's genuinely terrified of meeting strangers and, anyway, it's their house.

His brother-in-law has been the soul of thingummy and what's it, but he'll be glad when the three of them are on their own again. Just him and Mim and the kid.

Mim says the new flat will take at least another month before it's ready. But as they're working on it nights now as well as by day she says it should be possible for them to move in by September. Christ knows what they're doing to it. The ruddy place is taking longer than the Pyramids, but Castleton's quite happy to wait. The mention of September means Mim's taken the kid into her plans. She has admitted to a future for him. Hooray. Meanwhile, roll on the glorious First of August.

Paris is sweltering this last week of July. All doors to the terrace have been set open, shutters back, to catch the breeze from the garden. They have come up from St Eze for the kid's routine check-up, but chiefly, of course, for Crombie.

Everything's crossed for Crombie. 'Eat up, my duck,' says Castleton cheerfully.

The Dauphin is gazing myopically at the various dishes as if he has no idea what they are being offered to him for.

'Eat!' commands Marguerite. These are his favourite dishes. Dishes prepared especially for him. 'Now serve yourself at once! D'you hear?'

Poor old Mim. Still trying to keep it up. In the end she serves him from her plate: 'Là! Mange-moi ça! That little you must eat!'

But he just sits there smiling at them. The dining-room feels wonderfully cool. There is a mingled scent of fruit and flowers and where the air from the garden meets the heavier air from the room the rainy smell of watered grass.

'Eat it up, ducky,' says Castleton. He seems to have forgotten how to use his fork or how to swallow. At last his mother calls out: 'Oh, leave it! Starve if you want to! Since that is what you are aiming for!'

He gets down from his chair and stands there vaguely. 'What is the matter now?' demands his mother.

He doesn't want to go to the park any more.

There is no need to. Nobody forces him. The principal thing is that he eats his lunch.

'I don't want to go.'

'Come here, ducky,' says Castleton.

He goes and puts his wet face against Castleton's. 'Oh, my God,' says Marguerite impatiently, 'have you seen something in the park that frightened you?'

He begins, in a rambling sort of way: 'There was a little dog. It was under some leaves.'

'And then? What happened to the dog? I suppose it was dead?' remarks his mother.

He nods wordlessly.

'Oh, mon dieu, moumou,' Marguerite says. 'If you are going to make a scene for every animal that dies. Nothing lives for ever, you know.' She asks him: 'Are you going to finish your lunch or not?'

No. He doesn't want any more.

Then Gustave will take his napkin and he can go to bed. 'You can't expect Papa to eat his lunch with you on his knee.'

'It's all right, Mim. Let him get over it.'

There is nothing to get over. 'He will see such sights every day, and if he wasn't such a fool he would know it.'

George murmurs sickly: 'It had no head.'

Marguerite shrugs. 'Someone had cut it off, voilà tout. There are cruel people everywhere. Not everyone is as mad about animals as you. At nine years of age you should know that. Really, George, if I tell Bienville you are still such a crybaby he'll be disgusted with you.'

'There were so many flies.'

Naturally. There are always flies with dead animals. 'I hope you didn't touch it. That's all we need now, for you to catch an infection. Marcel has no business to let you go near these messes. He can count himself lucky not to get slung out.'

'No, Mimi, please,' begs George. His nurse has come to fetch him. He's so light now she just lifts him up and carries him off to bed like a child of four. Castleton can't bear to look, but Marguerite calls after him: 'Stop howling! D'you hear me? Or I will beat you like a carpet!'

Poor old Mim. She still keeps this phrase on her lips for comfort, like a dead fag on the lip of an ex-heavy

smoker. She's been marvellous with the kid ever since
they came to Paris. All the excesses of Vol. I a thing of
the past.

Vol. I is Castleton's name for life with the Sioux before
they came back to France from the States. Those awful
three months in New Orleans when Mim had tried to
bully her chap into instant integration with his latest stepfather by means too dirty even for Benoir. He had
actually ganged up with Castleton for a period to get her
to toe the line.

Poor old Breadcrumb.

'What did you say?'

Breadcrumb. That's what she'd told him once her
father used to call her.

'Really?'

Yes, really. 'Ma petite mie de pain,' her old man used
to call her. 'It's a play on words. Ho, ho,' Castleton says.

'Darling old Breadcrumb,' says Castleton. He takes her
in his arms and holds her for a bit. She waits quite
patiently for him to let her go, but occupies herself with
the re-pinning of a brooch.

'Thanks awfully,' says Castleton, letting her go. Still,
he feels fairly bright. He's thinking of next Friday.

'What is next Friday?' Marguerite wants to know.

'August the first,' says Castleton.

'Is that some special day?'

Castleton tells her. 'Oh, that,' says Marguerite. Never
mind. She's probably still a bit depressed over her chap
at lunch. Admittedly, forgetting his English like that is
frightfully depressing. He doesn't feel it quite so much
himself because he has got his omens. He has only started
to collect them lately. But he already has some good ones.

Benoir's tacit agreement that, even at this stage, it's still worth anybody's while to call in Crombie is one. And young Benoir's persistent absenteeism throughout his cousin's illness. That's a frightfully good omen. Stands up to all the tests, that does. Every day now Castleton has been asking away : 'I say, *what* about young Benoir?'

'What about him?' is the invariable reply.

He risks a bit more. 'You'd think he'd have the decency to show up once in a while. Seeing as *'ow*,' Castleton says, 'he's supposed to be devoted to his cousin.'

'Bienville is on his honeymoon,' says Marguerite coldly.

'He might at least phone,' Castleton says boldly.

She shrugs.

'Perhaps he doesn't realize how ill George is,' says Castleton, risking all at last.

She makes no comment. If she has understood the meaning behind his question she makes no sign. He waits for her to say something. If she doesn't speak now he can confidently put young Benoir back in the collection. She doesn't speak. God bless young Benoir. If George was worse he'd be here in a flash, honeymoon or no honeymoon. Castleton knows. He has developed quite a soft spot for young Benoir. He almost hopes it's mutual. He asks suddenly : 'Mim, is George like his father?'

'No, why d'you ask?'

'Oh, I don't know. He's nothing like you, is he?'

She says nothing.

'Does it upset you to talk about it?'

Not in the least. She would be delighted if George were like his father. Unfortunately Monsieur has elected to take after her mother. Armand is in despair.

'Why is he?'

'Why is he what?'

In despair. Castleton isn't in despair. He's got next Friday to look forward to. 'What's old Armand in despair about, darling?'

She answers shortly: 'Armand loved our mother to the exclusion of anyone else. I have already explained this whole thing to you, Vincent,' says Marguerite impatiently.

'So you have,' Castleton says, 'in Vol. I.'

'Comment?'

Never you mind, thinks Castleton. He's as pleased as punch with her answer. Not a word about death. It was a loaded question and she might have come back with all sorts of hideous answers. But she didn't. Another omen to him.

'Are you going to sit with George, Vincent?' Marguerite asks.

He doesn't know, 'Shall I?'

'It's as you wish.'

'He's changed, hasn't he?' Castleton says.

In what way? She asks him coldly: 'What is the matter this time, Vincent?' She is perfectly willing to pull her son up herself, but resents the least criticism from others.

Castleton says it wouldn't hurt him to thank the servants once in a while.

'What for?'

Show his appreciation a bit. 'They do so much for him.'

'Don't be ridiculous.' In her opinion they are already overcompensated for what they do.

'Get off,' says Castleton. He says, 'I'll go up later. I

don't seem able to cheer him up like I used to, poor old love.'

'Are you surprised? He has found out you are as fallible as the rest of us, voilà tout.'

Well, ta very much. Castleton says: 'Still, he does seem a lot better, don't you think? In himself, I mean.'

In himself? What is that supposed to mean?

'It means he's more himself. *In* himself,' says Castleton briskly. In fact, if Crombie okays him next Friday they might pop along to Antibes and join Cecil and Co for a few days. They've got a villa and Cecil says the bathing's terrific. 'What d'you think, darling?'

Marguerite thinks it is an idea to which she doesn't want to give any thought at all.

Well. Nice to know.

'I'll see you later, then, Vincent.'

'What are you doing now?'

Now? She is going to George.

How about afterwards? He thought they might have coffee together on the terrace first.

She has some correspondence to attend to. If he wants coffee he has only to order it.

'What about you?'

She has a fitting for 3.45 at her couturier.

'I say. It's all go, isn't it?' Castleton says.

6

In Benoir's Fairyland

He walks out on to the terrace for coffee. He is the only one who wants any it seems.

Monsieur Benoir is still in his office, Gustave informs him. He even had his lunch sent in, in order to be able to continue with his work. In Gustav's opinion the patron works too hard.

'Does he an' all? What's he work at?' Castleton wants to know. His mind is still running on Mim's mood.

It's politically induced, of course, because her chap's in direct line for everything. Mim had once told him that in the event of George's death the whole works go to Bienville. This was yonks ago, but he remembers it because of the way in which she'd said: 'As my immediate family choose to die like flies, I suppose it's a possibility one must face.'

He had been flabbergasted, but that was in Vol. I and goes to show what he's got used to since.

Le Patron works at his clinics. Gustave is quite astonished that Monsieur doesn't know this. It's an immense organization. The whole of the second floor at the back of the Ritz has been converted into offices solely to deal with this work.

'No, really?'

Most certainly. Monsieur has only to visit the second floor to satisfy himself. Gustave can promise him, 'Monsieur will be surprised.'

Monsieur might well be, come to that. Here is a totally new aspect of his playboy brother-in-law, whom Castleton had always pictured without a care in the world, apart from his rotten sister and lousy son, and who up till this moment has led, in Castleton's imagination, a delightfully louche existence divided between his various mistresses and many homes.

St Cloud. Mal Choisi, La Taquineuse. St Eze and the incomparable Ritz.

The incomparable Ritz, which Castleton has always thought of as Benoir's Fairyland, a place where mayfly companies of guests perpetually meet, part, and come together again, where nothing can happen that isn't amusing or chic, he now must think of as something totally different. A formidable complex, part cathedral, part office block, housing a holy project, raised in devotional piety to perpetuate the memory of his mother.

Well, I'll be blowed.

Castleton decides to take a look at it. It's nearly four o'clock and he doesn't want to go back to the bank. It's probably to do with his present life at home, but he doesn't like the Paris office very much.

Gustave is asking: 'Will Monsieur take a liqueur or some brandy?'

Neither, thanks. Castleton says he'll be going in directly. Meanwhile he can drink his coffee looking down at a vast parterre of scarlet salvia, a flood of roaring reds and shrieking greens stampeding past the whole length of the terrace to drop wildly, terrace by terrace, almost into the Seine.

This seems to be the favourite flower of his singular brother-in-law. There are more of them in front of the Ritz where powerful basinsfull flare in the centre court-yard, generating a hellish glow. Everywhere else the gardens have been charmingly laid out, a miniature Versailles of marble benches and statues with half-wild brakes of roses and bosky groves of Spanish acacia. A toile de jouy landscape designed for games of love, full of the sounds of water and a perpetual calling down of doves.

It's glorious July weather and the rocking wands of hundreds of buddleias are candied with a coating of flies and butterflies.

Gustave remarks sadly : 'It's a thousand pities petit monsieur can't benefit more from all this sun.'

'Still, he looks better, don't you think?' asks cunning Castleton, missing nary a chance to sound anyone out.

Most certainly, and now they have this new specialist to look forward to. Gustave declares : 'He could change the whole picture for us all.'

'Oh, absolutely.' It's an enormous relief to be able to talk to simple souls from Vol. I like Gustave, who hold no thoughts beyond those uttered and who clearly would prefer to believe in Crombie than in that other eventuality that so far nobody has mentioned, let alone discussed.

'A tout à l'heure, alors.' He takes leave of his pal the butler, and, skirting Benoir's Styx, whose lurid waves are now being disagreeably agitated by some invisible agent like a ground wind, he enters the Ritz by the back and takes the lift straight up to the legendary second floor.

Might as well take a look while waiting for August One.

He is immediately ushered, by staff he has never seen before, into a sunny, spacious office. Papers, journals, cigarettes are placed at his disposal.

Through a glass wall he can see his brother-in-law in another spacious office. He's seated at an enormous desk, full of vari-coloured telephones, speaking into a white one. Not a word can be heard. The whole place has been sound-proofed.

A secretary goes in and soundlessly announces Castleton, and a whole rose drops silently on to the desk at the silently opened door.

His brother-in-law is vivaciously beckoning him to come in : 'Be with you in one moment, fella.'

More papers, journals and cigarettes are placed at Castleton's disposal.

The quiet room is very sunny. His smiling brother-in-law is smoking steadily. He's listening calmly to someone on the line who appears not to want any answers. Probably Bienville. For some time now Castleton has noticed a coolness between Benoir and his son.

He opens a copy of *Country Life*. There is the usual spread of buck teeth and shooting sticks. Castleton country.

'Be here and make it fast,' smiling Benoir is saying.

Bienville.

Hepplewhite chairs. Two carvers, ten diners. He doesn't care for Hepplewhite much. Pictures of pictures by Stubbs. Jolly. The Grosvenor House Fair. Carolean and early Queen Anne pewter, some of it very fine. If anyone fancies pewter. Christie's are advertising a beautiful little pair of Chelsea figures. Also a monstrous monkey orchestra by Meissen. He's wondering who'd buy the bloody thing when a voice he barely recognizes as Benoir's says viciously : 'Get the hell over, hear me? Get the lead out of your pants.'

It's Bienville all right.

Benoir is patently livid, but Castleton grins. He feels very warm towards young Benoir for sticking out for his rights. He hopes he goes on enjoying his honeymoon for many weeks to come. If there was any anxiety over his cousin's condition he'd be here like a shot, so jolly good luck to young Benoir, purveyor of Castleton's best cherished omen.

He cheerfully studies a boring spray brooch by van Cleef and Arpels. Fine diamond and pearl with clip ear-rings to match. Just the job for his darling sister-in-law for Christmas. If Cecil hasn't already bought 'em for his blessed girl.

Benoir has rung off. He is full of apologies for keeping Castleton waiting. He sounds a bit more French than usual but otherwise quite normal. There is absolutely no fear of his forgetting all his English as he explains the second-floor setup to Castleton.

The second floor of the Ritz is quite a place. Inner offices lead to outer offices. Reference and TV rooms. A separate exchange and a charming bijou cinema which, Castleton is told, is only used for a certain type of film. The only thing left unexplained is the picture which hangs directly opposite Benoir's desk.

And how he can bear to look at it passes Castleton's comprehension.

It's a portrait of his mother by the Brazilian artist Cabral, painted at the time when her disease was finally doing her in.

She's the image of Mim's chap and as full of it as he is. Even her furs are full of it. By digesting snowy skin in snowy skins, Cabral has managed to fix the actual moment of dissolution.

Castleton takes one look at his late mother-in-law and turns away. Those furs have already started to make rubbish of his omens. He has got to get out of this office. Benoir says tranquilly : 'If you're going to see puss I'll come with you. I have to collect my Marie before those two have giggled themselves silly.'

In the lift they chat of this and that.

'Baudouin is coming to see puss tonight,' his smiling brother-in-law informs him.

'Oh, really?' Baudouin Benoir is Mim's younger brother, a wreck of a young man in a clever electric chair. The Sioux call him the Skeleton for obvious reasons. The Skeleton is very angry with himself and hates almost everyone except Mim, and if it wasn't for her he would probably make away with himself. But Mim adores him – though, to be fair, she loves Benoir best.

Castleton hasn't seen his younger brother-in-law since his wedding when he had found him unattractive and impossible to buddy up. There is another reason for his dislike. The Skeleton is the one who didn't die. He is the living picture of what it looks like to be cured of an incurable disease.

Castleton asks his brother-in-law abruptly. 'Is Bienville coming tonight?'

Benoir has no idea. He announces calmly: 'I have washed my hands of that case.'

That's all right. That's for the grandstand. Routine stuff, no more alarming than any previous answer to this question, and it explains the late row on the blower. Benoir adores his ruddy son, but like all the Sioux he's inclined to set impossibly lofty standards.

About Mim's older brother Castleton thinks: He's an awfully decent stick. Since the thing has taken on serious proportions he's had it from all of us. Talks. Negotiations. Decisions. You name it, he's taken it on. Poor chap, his sex life must be a shambles just now with all our claims and clamourings. Though, knowing Benoir, he's probably thought up ways and means.

Castleton suddenly grins. He has made two decisions. He will stop looking into the tea leaves and he will trust his smiling brother-in-law.

As they leave the lift, a secretary accosts them. 'Monsieur Viv is on the line, Monsieur Benoir. He asks to speak with you again.'

To this Benoir makes no reply whatsoever.

7

Pretty Marie

There is tremendous excitement going on in the bedroom where the Dauphin and his little aunt are racing each other to finish a king-size jigsaw puzzle. Pretty Marie is smoking like a chimney. She is a terrifically heavy smoker and the only person privileged to smoke in the Dauphin's bedroom. Two facts which never fail to tickle Castleton.

'Alors, Marie, ça va?'

He greets his little sister-in-law, kissing her hand and then on either cheek. She smiles at him silently from under curiously level brows. She hardly speaks a word of English. He likes her very much.

She is the little model Benoir loves to experiment with in dress. Just now he's in the middle of a Kirschner phase and spends whole afternoons looking through swatches of charmeuse and triple ninon in all the thé dansant colours of tango, azalea and flame. Very Vie Parisienne.

Bundles of silver fox skins impeccably matched, snowy Arctics, black Alaskas, teamed to achieve the magpie classic of the twenties, jaguar and monkey hair, mournful and glycerined, for her amazing capes and hats.

At the moment Marie's lingerie is made exclusively from crêpe-de-Chine, scattered, Mim tells him, with 'toutes les fleurs de Nice'.

'Les zolies roses, les violettes de Parme, et beaucoup, beaucoup de thouthis!' said awful Mim, making a moue with her mouth full of salad. Marie lisps slightly.

Every stitch of Marie's wardrobe is made in France to designs from the great ateliers of Paris. Only her gloves and shoes are made in Spain. This is a fact which Benoir quite seriously deplores. He is extremely patriotic when it comes to placing orders. All the same, he is convinced that only Albafura of Madrid still understands the art of working in fine leather.

He is intensely proud of Marie's hands and feet and has recently given her a tiny watch by Fabergé to wear round her ankle. Old Mim says it doesn't matter where she wears it as, at thirty-five, Marie still hasn't learnt to tell the time.

Every day is Marie's birthday for Benoir, who showers her with vanity cases and cigarette holders, museum pieces of Art Déco worked over gold in coloured enamels. He buys her slave bangles of green nephrite and mauve jade and a charming amulet of brilliants and red coral to swing on a chain made from a single elephant's hair.

Every finger of Marie's hands is loaded with rings, but her nails are kept surprisingly short and trimmed quite square, like a boy's. Benoir has an antipathy to long and brightly varnished nails.

Mim, of course, has a theory that her sister-in-law looks like one of those plaster figurines offered to tourists from wayside stands at Lourdes. The answer to that is a large lemon, but Benoir cracks down on her smartly: 'If my wife has no appeal for you it's because you understand nothing about purity.'

Like Napoleon, Benoir is very hot on purity in women, and prizes it no end.

For Castleton Marie is a doll dressed all in white, long-legged and pigeon-toed on a white sofa. Her smiling face is charmingly painted, with touches of dry rouge under her rounded chin and at the corners of her great Laurencin eyes. Benoir has excelled himself this afternoon – under her simple white frock the clocks on Marie's white silk stockings reveal themselves as marvels of Parisian fantasy.

Charming Marie. Castleton likes her very much.

'You'll have to shout, she's deaf,' explains the Dauphin importantly, who sees himself as her manager. He promises his stepfather in a shriek. 'I'll greet you later when I have vanquished my auntie.'

There are boos of protest when Benoir takes over and calmly completes the last corner of the forest of Rambouillet for them.

'O, how he has spoiled it all for us!'

'Ah non, tu sais, Armand,' murmurs Marie.

Her nephew consoles her: 'There was only the green part left. It wasn't very amusing.'

Benoir points out complacently: 'It's the green part that counts.'

Marie is gazing at George expectantly as usual. They are in league over everything, though he is mostly in the lead. Their fuss over the puzzle was all put on. They adore Benoir to do their puzzles for them. Instantly both are clamouring to start a new one.

The Dauphin says resourcefully: 'If we all muck in it

will be finished in 'arf a mo'.' He is consulting the lid.
'It's a London scene, don't you know. Avec la Tamise
and 'ouses of Parliament.'

His English has miraculously been restored to him. 'If
we hurry we can finish it before Mama comes home,'
announces the Dauphin, ambitiously starting to deal out
pieces.

He is quite blatant in his favours. All the scarlet bits
go to his aunt to make up London buses, while Castleton
is thrown a wet-looking heap of London pavement. Only
Benoir stands firm against all master-minding. He
announces his intention of withdrawing his wife from the
royal bedside forthwith and substituting his long-suffering
brother-in-law, 'who, by the way, you haven't greeted
yet.'

George calls out instantly : 'Bonjour, mon pa. We met
at lunch, I think?'

'We did, indeed.'

George asks curiously : 'What was I howling for?
D'you know? I have forgotten.'

'Never you mind,' says Castleton.

'D'you like your new name, Pa? Pa, my own pa?'
enquires his stepson.

Castleton says he likes it very much.

'Tantan and I invented it for you. We think it suits
you.'

He will have to obtain official permission from Mimi
first before he can use it. But, as far as one can see, that
should present no serious difficulty.

'In any case it is the only solution. For everyone,' says
George who is referring to the fight he'd had with Mim
early in Vol. I when the question of what to call Castle-

ton had cropped up. Mim had insisted upon papa, and George had flatly refused to give up his own father's name. Apparently something of the sort had happened when Mim had married her second husband Governor Davis.

Both wars were lost, of course, but only after Mim had thrown in everything and literally licked her small opponent hollow, so taking it all in all, Castleton considers the victory had gone to his rum stepson.

Except for the briefest period after his defeat, George had succeeded in never once calling him anything.

At the moment his rum stepson and Marie are taking regretful leave of one another. They appear to have had a whale of an afternoon. The remains of an elaborate tea for two are still on a trolley.

Anyone who still fancies tea, George assures them, has only to press the bell when all necessary equipment will be brought. At the risk of disappointing somebody, Benoir is more concerned to have the tea-things cleared as soon as possible. 'If Mama comes home and sees this clutter she'll want to know a reason.'

'O, yes, she will not half,' agrees George warmly. 'She has an enquiring mind, my mother.' He watches the trolley being wheeled through the door. 'Au 'voir, my own dear darling petite tantan-chérie. It has been lovely seeing you. I love you very much.'

'You will be seeing her at dinner,' his uncle assures him. 'I would like you two to rest before you meet again.' He is leading his Marie from the room by the hand.

'Attendez. I still have to give her back her sweet little doggie,' calls out George. He produces a tiny black and white Japanese spaniel from under the bedclothes and hands it to his aunt. 'My bed is full of animals these days,' he informs his stepfather happily.

'Really? Does mummy know?' enquires a staggered Castleton.

O, yes. And when he's quite better he fully intends to have a little dog of his own. Whatever that bunch at the Clinic have to say. '*Mummy* has promised me,' George adds saucily.

'I see,' says Castleton, uneasily. This total reversal of Mim's no pets policy has winded him completely. 'What about Bertil and Dagobert?' Castleton wants to know. Better make a joke of it before he starts crying woe again. 'Have you got them in bed with you, too?'

'Oh, you are funny,' shrieks George. Bertil and Dago-bert are guard dogs at the Ritz. Horned, stove-black devils of Dobermans the Dauphin dotes on. He is blowing kisses at his aunt's little dog: 'Au 'voir, my little Miss. You have been very sweet. I hope I shall see you at dinner as well?'

He will see them all at dinner. His uncle informs him: 'Your Uncle Beau is coming, by the way.'

The Skeleton. 'O, my Redeemer, I am not madly keen.' (The Skeleton is not persona grata with his nephew.) George asks: 'Will Vivi be here too, Uncle Benoir? Shall I see him tonight, my cousin?'

Castleton holds his breath.

Benoir thinks it extremely unlikely that Viv will show tonight.

Castleton breathes out.

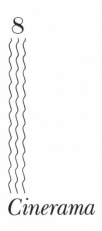

8

Cinerama

The minute they are alone George bursts out: 'O, I am perfectly fed up of that Viv. I think he is the louse of all the world. He never comes to see me.'

He's on his honeymoon. Castleton suggests, 'If you're going to look at films you'd better put your specs on.'

'Well, I am sick of Viv's honeymoon,' George tells him. 'And, for a second thing, if it interests you, I am sick of my specs as well.'

'Don't you want to see a film, then?'

Usually he's mad about movies and spends most of his afternoons after his nap looking at splendid collections of nature films on a specially angled screen. The Amazon – a vast skid-pan of shining pink mud, solid as a road, cutting through forest, mile upon mile, as far as the eye can reach. An equatorial mud flood, gay with the corpses of a thousand toucans and sunbirds and cordon-bleus, while every so often a limp python or a jaguar comes trundling past the Dauphin's appreciative gaze.

'Il est formidable, ce fleuve.'

Snow gums beside the rushing Snowy River. The keen toothed Victorian Alps.

The Dauphin says off-handedly: 'By the way, I am seeing your doctor on Friday. He is supposed to be Australian too, or something.'

'Yes. Don't you want to go?' He absolutely loathes the Clinic.

George answers in a new listless voice: 'O, they'll get me there somehow, don't you know. Dead or alive.' He doesn't sound very interested.

'Get on,' says Castleton, giving him a kiss. They are looking at skies plated with cloud floes against the delicate Arctic blue, as trillions of trilliums shoulder themselves out of the snow in the spring woods of Canada.

'My God,' observes the Dauphin cryptically. He's either still thinking about the Clinic or about his cousin.

A whole sunset of flamingoes detaches itself suddenly from the sky and flaps heavily over the grass green African lake to roost, or whatever it is flamingoes do, behind the Dauphin's bed.

'O, my Redeemer.' He's getting on his own nerves by calling out incessantly. By the time Mt Egmont is on the screen he merely says politely: 'It's Fuji Yama, that? It must be quite nice down there in Japan.' He isn't really looking. The crude, bright, travel poster colours of New Zealand seem to offend him.

'Do your eyes hurt you, darling?'

For the moment, George considers he could say that they do. He has slipped down in bed and pulled the covers round him.

'Ducky.'

'Yes, what d'you want?' He throws his spectacles out of bed and closes his eyes.

'Ducky,' says Castleton.

He opens an eye and smiles.

It isn't good to sleep too much during the day. 'Don't go to sleep now, darling, or you'll spoil your rest at night.' He's taken to wandering at night for no particular reason. Mim said she'd found him in her bathroom once or twice.

'So don't sleep now,' Castleton says.

'O, then I will not,' promises the Dauphin, anxious not to be kept from his treat.

He is asleep immediately. He attacks sleep like a meal he has been ravening for.

Castleton turns the music off, but the pictures go on showing themselves silently on the screen, whole landscapes revolving slowly like models at a dress show.

Black swans assembling on the Swan River estuary, rocking and knocking up against the sunset, black as coal barges.

Castleton switches the picture off and makes for the door.

'Where are you going?' demands the Dauphin, instantly sitting up in bed fresh as a daisy.

'Hullo. You've been asleep,' says Castleton.

'It's what I like to do lately,' explains the Dauphin kindly. 'It's nice, don't you know. I can recommend it.'

He seems vastly refreshed and eager to talk again.

'If you like, we can yack,' proposes the Dauphin.

They talk about flowers. He knows all the names.

'Aren't you clever?'

'When I was young I used to be,' the Dauphin dis-

claims the praise rather gloomily. He quizzes his stepfather severely : 'What is your favourite flower?'

Daffodils.

'Then they are mine,' the Dauphin claims them
firmly.

'Ce sont les narcisses jaunes,' explains Castleton.

He knows them. He has seen fleurs de coucou many
times. 'And you needn't speak French.' Mme Li, the
friend of his Uncle Benoir, always buys them. But only
from street vendors. On the streets they do them up like
pineapples with tufts of leaves on top. 'She says they
remember her of when she was a little girl.'

'Remind her,' says Castleton.

'Well, that's the whole thing,' George agrees warmly.
'She comes from Normandy, you see.'

The favourite flower of his Uncle Benoir is freesia. At
Christmas he will fill the house with them so you can
hardly breathe. It's quite delightful.

George says : 'I hope we'll be in Paris for Christmas.
It is such fun. At Réveillon my Uncle Benoir gives a most
splendid supper for one hundred people in the Grande
Orangerie.' At least, only fifty of them are people, the rest
are children. George says dramatically : 'Fifty kids all
talking at once, can y'all imagine the net result?'

On top of this they are all Parisian children. They
will give sass as soon as look at you. 'Also the Orangerie
is full of birds, so you will have an idea of all the screaming and whistling.'

The supper itself is splendid. George says it's not
possible to depict how beautiful it all looks. It seems there
is a special Sèvres service and some damn tablecloth or
other that took two years to embroider.

'I *say*,' says Castleton.

The Dauphin reports happily : 'Two of the embroideresses went blind.'

There is a huge table shaped like a horse-shoe for the grownups and another only for children. 'We are allowed to sing and make jokes all through the supper because it is our Saviour's birthday. And at dessert we all change places and sit beside the grownup we like best. I always choose to sit between Mama and Uncle Benoir, but this year I shall sit next to you. You'll have to pay me six dragées. Three pink, three white. That's for your place at the table. It's a forfeit. Everyone who isn't in the family has to pay. After you've bought your place you are no longer a stranger. It isn't difficult.' The Dauphin says magnanimously : 'I will be there to help you.'

'Thanks,' Castleton says. 'I should shut up now, ducky.'

He has talked so much his English has started to go and he's rushing to get it all in while it lasts.

'That trash Viv will have to buy Mlle Elaine's place for her this year.' It's the first time he'll sit at the grownups' table. 'Big deal.' George says bitterly : 'I won't care. All he does is throw bread in everyone's face and annoy the servants.'

George says : 'I guess my Uncle Benoir will lend us Tante Marie to be Queen at our table. She's the same size as us, and anyway she's about one million times better than my stinking cousin.'

George says : 'Everyone goes to mass at Réveillon, even my Uncle Benoir will go to please my Tante Marie. Only my Viv won't go. That fink !' calls George. Suddenly he is laughing uncontrollably about his cousin, 'I guess it would just about slay that fink to behave himself.'

George says: 'Oh, I just hope you will be able to see it, that's all.'

'Why not?' asks Castleton.

'Well, there is always something,' George says reasonably. He adds almost immediately: 'O, by the way, I saw my ex today.' He's talking about his former step-father, Mim's second husband, Governor Davis, for whom he has a predilection. 'He was polite,' the Dauphin tells him. 'We 'ad a chat.'

Castleton grins. The Sioux have achieved many marvels of organization, but this afternoon they have outdone themselves. He and his predecessor had actually been in the house together without so much as glimpsing each other. Luverly stuff. Particularly as the Dauphin always tells him everything.

'I thought it would amuse you,' calls out George, who is climbing back into his pit of sleep again. His voice sounds very far away. 'A tout à l'heure, mon pa. I'll see you at dinner.'

As Castleton leaves the room he walks into his wife, the ex-Mrs Davis who, with her usual directness, says: 'I hope you haven't been with moumou all this time, Vincent?'

' 'Fraid so,' Castleton says.

'You know he is supposed to rest before dinner. Had you forgotten or what?'

'Or what,' says Castleton promptly.

9

The Clinic

In the car he feels cold and lousy again. He can feel his mother's legs warm against his own under the rug. 'Mimi?'

'What? Sit up straight, George,' commands Marguerite. Her huge-brimmed hat shows off to perfection the discontented beauty of her mouth.

He pulls himself up with difficulty. He wants to know what is going to happen afterwards.

'After what?'

After this new man has examined him, George means.

What should happen? 'Sit straight, d'you hear? I won't tell you again.'

'Yes'm.' He wants her to say he won't have to stay on at the Clinic. O, if she will only tell him he can go home.

She says: 'Afterwards you will go home and eat your lunch as usual, voilà tout.'

'O, you are darling for me!' He throws both arms round her neck. 'O, Mimi, I adore you so!'

Looks like it! Marguerite calls out: 'Stupid thing! Look what you're doing with my hat!' She eyes him

sombrely under the enormous brim. That child! He is
falling to bits again!

'Give your legs here to me!'

He lifts them by turns into her lap while she sets him to
rights, grumbling loudly all the while. About his socks
which have fallen over his shoes. About his shoes which
are, as usual, falling off his feet. She threatens: 'I'll put
you into sabots stuffed with straw, mon vieux.' Perhaps
that will dissuade him from changing his measurements
every two days. 'It's quite idiotic to expect your boot-
maker to keep up indefinitely with this sort of nonsense.'

George coaxes: 'I am supposed to be getting fatter
soon, Mimi. Dr Meyer says it is quite on the cards.'

Dr Meyer will end by convincing them all. 'Cover your
bones up,' Marguerite says.

'No, truly. I will eat every single thing you put before
me,' promises George.

He will get a good smack if he doesn't. That is another
thing on the cards.

O, she is funning. George asserts stoutly: 'You can
do what you like with me. Whatever it is, I'll be sure to
like it.'

He needn't be so sure. 'You have been told to cover
yourself,' observes his mother.

He draws the rug up to his chin at once. Poor thing,
he's grateful because she has told him he is going home
after his examination. He has become suddenly very
quiet, feeling and fingering her hand under the covers.
That is because they are nearing the Clinic. She asks
him slyly: 'Are you howling, by any chance?'

'No, Mama,' George answers her politely.

Tiens, she could have sworn he was.

'No, Mama.' He is watching the street.

'Turn your head. Moumou! Cheeky thing!' That brat has thrown her completely by suddenly sticking his face under her hat. He remarks calmly: 'I told you twice I wasn't crying. If you still don't believe me, you can look for yourself.'

It could be Benoir talking. She's astounded every time at this change which has recently come over her son. Suddenly he will sound as if he was the grown-up and it is she who is the child. She asks him sharply: 'Are you trying to be impertinent?'

O, no, he is not. Truly. Only in the circs George rather feels it isn't any use to tell the truth. 'In the existing circs,' says George, 'and if you get my meaning.'

He has got those expressions from Vincent's man again. And after she had expressly forbidden the association. She accuses him point blank: 'D'you dare to tell me you would lie to me?'

It would make a change. 'D'abord I like your hat,' puts in the Dauphin neatly.

Little tramp. He'll soon change his tune. In three more minutes, even with this traffic, they'll be at the Clinic. They are already at the Etoile. She's delighted to see Monsieur has turned positively green. He's shivering like a little dog. Great tears are dripping off his chin. Good, he's her property again.

'Don't cry, my silly darling,' Marguerite tells him. 'I don't want you to cry.'

She's taking off his spectacles. His eyes are magnificent even with them on. Even with all this ironmongery she still has a splendid child. 'Alors, c'est fini?' demands Marguerite.

He lets her wipe his eyes. 'O, I do love you,' sobs George.

That's good because she has a secret for him. 'Pass me your ear,' says Marguerite.

She starts to whisper, pausing to kiss him, pausing to get her answers from his eyes. 'D'you understand what I'm saying? Moumou-without-your-goggles?' asks Marguerite.

He nods. Her perfume is blossoming magically for him like a fabulous tree. She puts her mouth to his ear again, whispering closely, cupping his ear with her hand so that not a syllable is lost.

'You are my precious little son. I love you so much, so much. I want you to be perfect. That's why I'm sometimes bad to you when you start trembling and bawling like a calf. You are to be perfect at your examination today. Perfect, d'you understand?'

That is their secret. It's strictly between them both. 'Will you do it for me?'

He nods.

'I love you,' says Marguerite.

He nods.

'Va t'en,' says Marguerite. She throws his spectacles at him. 'Here, put your hardware on, or I will catch it from the men again because of you.' Little force-ripe! So much for her famous declaration of love. She had been purposely cautious for fear of scaring him with it. In fact, nothing of the sort had happened. Monsieur had accepted her confession as calmly as he accepted the whole situation. It's clearly no news to that one to hear he's the centre of her universe.

They are almost at the Clinic and Monsieur is still

sitting with his spectacles in his hand. In fact it's not before Marcel is actually coming round to open the door that he can find the necessary energy to put them on his nose.

'Alors, on ne bouge pas, ou quoi?'

'In a minute, Mama.'

What is that supposed to mean?

It means that in a minute he will get out of the car. 'If I get out now I will fall on my face in the street and you won't like that, either.'

The barefaced cheek of that brat of hers! 'Move yourself,' orders Marguerite. But he stands his ground, persisting mulishly: 'No. You have ordered me not to cry so you will have to wait.'

That remains to be seen. She will enlist Deckers' help to supplement Marcel's to haul him out of the car and into the Clinic. If needs be they'll carry him in on a stretcher!

He is helped out with more difficulty than usual. Marguerite exclaims: 'It's taking forever!' What is the matter with that child? She tells her son: 'You are behaving like a ninety-year-old arthritic.'

'Yes'm, I'm sorry,' says George.

He's out on the pavement now, momentarily immobilized between the two men. Three grey-shawl'd pigeons are moving round and round the kerb in a close clockwork circle. He would like a moment to examine the dark, quiet borders of their folded wings, their naked feet, the neon pink and gold of their bright necks, but Mimi keeps pushing him from behind.

'Move!' He will see them again, his pigeons, later on

when he comes out of the Clinic. Or does he already see himself being carried out in his coffin?

'O, Mimi, look! They are kissing each other.' George insists you could almost put it they are all three making love!

He's playing for time, but she has already guessed his reason for standing still. 'My God, moumou, don't tell me you've developed another boil on your behind?' It's only two weeks since he had his last one. She accuses him of making a cult of it. 'You'll be turning up at your wedding with a boil on your tutu!' She predicts with relish: 'Your wife will leave you immediately!'

This idea amuses her mightily. It doesn't amuse her son whose immediate job is to walk up the Clinic steps in a way that will conceal from his mother the fact that his carbuncle has burst.

She is already racing up the steps to lay an authoritative finger on the bell. 'The sooner you make up your mind the sooner it will be over.'

The glass doors part noiselessly. She vanishes into the Clinic without a backward glance while Marcel and Deckers are still helping him negotiate the steps. He follows her into the foyer, demanding breathlessly: 'Who will be here, Mama? Will anyone from home be coming?'

Everyone will be here. As usual he has managed to disrupt everybody's day. Papa, Uncle and herself. The 'House Full' boards are out, his mother assures him.

'Will Viv be here, Mama?' presses George.

She points out briefly: 'Bienville is on his honeymoon.' And that is the very last question she intends to answer.

George complains loudly: 'O, he promised me! He's

put the shuck on me again. O, I am perfectly sick of that schmuck!'

She threatens him suddenly with her open hand. 'No dramas, d'you hear? Just let me catch you at it!'

Fortunately he's still child enough to be silenced by her gesture, because the whole Clinic seems to be converging on them. She takes one look at her son to see that he is behaving, before she dissociates herself from him completely.

Alerted by receptionist Frl Rene Kraus, the pneumatic figures of co-directors Walter Winkler and Dietrich Dieter-Zultz, the 'Michelin Men' as moumou calls them, are bowling rapidly towards Marguerite with widely welcoming smiles, while Dr Frieda Boss-Hart, resident physician of the children's wing, is bowing over her hand like a man, effecting boring introductions to personnel she has either never known or has been happy to forget.

What interests her at the moment is what has happened to Madeleine? She should be here to fetch moumou up to the flat.

Direktor Dieter-Zultz is beaming: 'And how is our friend Georges? I think you should be proud of your son, Mrs Castleton. He is a stalwart fellow. I think he enchoys to visit us here. He looks always so chirpy. To be sure, we like Georges to visit us also. Und so,' says Dieter-Zultz relentlessly, 'we come to the conclusion that the sentiment is mutual. I razzer think. Or no?' says Dieter-Zultz.

Marguerite glances at her son's face. If he had been addressed in Swahili he couldn't have understood less. She cuts further civilities by asking if her son's bonne has arrived yet?

'Of course, of course.'

'Most emphatically of course,' corroborates Herr Winkler. 'Und M. Benoir is here also, as well.'

'Und Mr Castleton,' puts in Dieter-Zultz. 'Needless to say.'

Quite needless. Herr Winkler adds that each and everyone is now simply and solely awaiting Mrs Castleton's presence at the apartment on the private ninth floor.

Dr Frieda sighs in ogreish aside: 'Mme Benoir – excuse me – Mrs Kastletohn is looking, as usual, sweet enough to eat. So tender! So tiny! Ach!'

Herr Winkler has laid a kindly trotter on George's shoulder. 'Und now I think our first and foremost plan will be for our famous fellow here to go and get ready for his examination. Aha! I see your bonne is already here to fetch you! This is quite famous! I think you are a thought reader, Mme Madeleine.'

Dieter-Zultz invites expansively: 'You can take your little friend upstairs, Mme Madeleine.' He tells Marguerite: 'A pity we have to part. But we have sadly to remember that Time Marches On.'

And not before time, thinks Marguerite, as Mammy takes charge of her son. My God, the difference in that child! One moment he looks like a tête-de-mort: the next he is laughing with Madeleine like a mad thing!

She calls out sharply: 'Moumou! Madeleine!' Those two are kissing in the lift like lovers!

'FE-NO-ME-NAL!' pronounces Herr Winkler, who is all for high spirits and youthful jinks. In the meantime they can adjourn for a little chat before the good doctors arrive.

Dr Boss-Hart points out with some asperity that the doctors are already here.

'Zo?' Direktor Zultz is in the act of ushering Marguerite into a lift. 'Mr Keith Crombie is here as well?'

Dr Boss-Hart ripostes snarkily: 'I have just said *all* the doctors, Herr Dieter-Zultz. This comprises docteurs Meyer et Bonvin, Professeur Courvoisier *and* Mr Keith Crombie from Australia.'

'Zozo. Goodgood.' In this case M. Benoir has probably already had a chat with them. 'A little chat?' suggests Herr Winkler wistfully. 'I razzer think?'

More talks! Marguerite thinks, as if they could possibly lead anywhere.

Benoir and she have already agreed between them that moumou is not to be subjected to further 'severe' treatment – least of all surgery. Of course, Benoir is putting on this act with Crombie for Vincent's benefit. Probably he has already smelled our marriage is on the rocks and he's afraid I could revert to being his sole responsibility in case of moumou's death. Poor man, it's not surprising he isn't keen to have this as well as everything he already has on his plate.

Marguerite smiles and as one man Dieter-Zultz, Winkler and Boss-Hart smile as well.

She is suddenly furious with her brother for subjecting her to this Alpine ordeal every time she shows her nose in this place. For reasons best known to himself the entire administrative side of the Paris clinic is now in the hands of the Swiss. It's probably another of those tedious experiments Benoir is always making.

He has already informed her that the new one at Rabat

will be interdenominational. As if she cares what he does with his clinics except, if he has any ideas of calling it, or any future clinics, posthumously in moumou's name, she will have the greatest pleasure in holding back permission.

The Georges-Marie Armand Benoir. She will fight against that to the last drop of her blood.

When he was little, thinks Marguerite, he had belonged exclusively to his father, and she had had the biggest struggle after Georges' death to annex him. Poor thing, he'd had more smacks than kisses from her at the time, but in the end he had capitulated, and now he is her exclusive property.

If she had her way he would never have been brought here today to see this famous Australian specialist no one in Paris seems to have heard of. But, of course, it was Vincent's wish, so Benoir is indulging it to the full.

Marguerite thinks contemptuously : Benoir stepping up his programme of appeasement in the time left before moumou croaks and she is on the market again. It's not true, but lately she has taken such a hate against the men. Both of them. One is as bad as the other. They play into each other's hands. She's thoroughly sick of this police state which they run between them, and in which she can't even do as she likes with her own child.

Well, let this Australian examine her son. If it turns out to be unpleasant, all the better. The men have ordered it so if it puts the child against them she won't mind. But if this character says one word about treatment she's going to put her foot down. And she will do it before those two oppositionists have time to open their mouths.

The lift doors slide open to reveal the bright white light of the top floor. Alors, allons parler boutique.

The Michelin Men bow as she steps out of the lift, while Dr Boss-Hart, prior to pounding lab-wards in blinding new sneakers, barks a cheery aufwiedersehn, showing a dark and doggish smile lit with gold.

The Michelin Men are gallantly preparing to see Marguerite to the door of the flat. They are already saying things like: 'Our heart-felt wishes for the examination'. She turns and literally runs from the lot of them.

Alone in their swift lift, George and Mammy are killing themselves over everything. The Michelin Men, Boss-Hart, and their hilarious stopatthetopflooronly lift.

'Baby, one time dis elevator sure goin' *kerpow* thru' de ceilin'! Hey, you evuh grab yo'sel' an eyeful of dat big Boss-feller? Man, she got five o'clock shadder!' Mammy shrieks.

They fall into each other's arms, intoning: 'Got five o'clock, six o'clock, rock-aroun'-de-clock shadder!'

'You black taranchla, you!' Mammy is wiping streaming eyes. They're at the top and she's still laughing, but he's already holding his hand out for his key.

'Be quick! Silly thing! Pass me my key!' Uncle Benoir has had one specially cut for him because he had stood his last tests so well. It's just about the highest honour you can have. He wants to open his door with his own private key.

'Moumou! Bad thing! You ask polite, now, else you don' get no key!' She's already taking it out of her bag. 'Whyn't you leave me open it fer you, baby? Y'all ain't have de strent'.'

'Let me! Let me!' He is stamping at her with both feet. 'I want to open my door!'

She hands it to him. 'Cain't even see to fin' the lock, even.'

But he commands her furiously: 'Be quiet! You are not to speak whiles I open my door.'

'Says who?'

'I say. You are my servant,' George says. 'When I have opened my door I will kiss you.'

He is intent on finding the lock and turning the key with his weak hands. Now. He has opened it. He throws the key back. 'Here, keep it in your bag. No one is to touch my key but you. Compris?'

'Yessir.'

'Say what you are.'

'I am your servant.' She thinks, that bob-cat. He gettin' to be the walkin' image of Madame.

'Mado.'

'What, baby?'

Nothing. Just Mado. Now he has unlocked his door he doesn't want to go in.

'Come on, now, baby. We gotta get you all fixed up. Don't, Madame will want to know a reason.'

He walks into the lobby. His mood lifts when he sees a favourite carpet of his from Neuilly has been laid down. Hoopoes on swags of lilacs and roses. The cock-birds in their war-bonnets swing boldly amongst the French greys and mauves.

He stands there studying it for a long time. When he has traced it carefully round a corner he observes: 'I like this carpet. I am going home for lunch, you know.'

'Who say?' The last time he had told her that, he had had to stay.

'You can take it from me,' says George.

She doesn't dare say more. Instead she tries again to make him move. 'You ain't took your coat off even.' But he has spotted a nest amongst the lilac sprays.

'Moumou.'

A hoopoe nestful of hoopoe eggs. It's making him smile. He lifts his head, suddenly finished with the carpet. 'Okay, I'm coming. What are you fussing about?' All one hears is her voice. 'If it interests you, my carbuncle has burst, so you will have the honour of changing my chemise.'

She will do anything if only he will start to undress. 'Any time now that Boss-fella she gonna push her museau aroun' dat do'.'

He disappears into the bedroom, remarking: 'Well, anyway, I am going to take a bath.'

She draws it for him. The telephone rings. Mammy calls out: 'Now, wut I tol' you? Wut I jus' say?' She comes back from the telephone. 'You don't hafta go down, Dr Meyer say –'

He is not in the bath.

'Moumou! Where you at? You listening wut I say?' She comes into the bedroom. 'They all comin' up or some-thin', gonna xamine you here or somethin', Dr Meyer say. . . .'

He is lying on the bed fully dressed.

'Moumou! All this time you ain' even start to un-dress!' Mammy threatens: 'You want I should fetch Madame?'

'Yes. I like her,' says George.

'Lip. Trouble is you too spoil. Look this whole beautiful apartment le Patron done made over. One whole
floor jus' only for you.'

'Yes. I hate it,' says George.

'Key an' everthing.'

'Yes. I hate it,' says George.

Petit bougre. She starts to undress him as if he were
a sacred effigy. He's so puny you could take all of his
clothes off without undoing a button. His legs are black and
blue with all them piqûres they keep on jabbing into him.
That bubon on his bottom looks real mean. A volcano
with three gaily coloured fumeroles erupting a tallowy
pus. The main crater is an extinct-looking brown that is
somehow worst of all. Better get a towel. Lay it under.

'What are you crying for?' asks George.

'Nobody cryin'. Just gonna fetch me a towel.'

He grabs her hand.

'Come on, you let me,' Mammy says. The front-door
buzzer goes and, at the same time, somebody puts a key
into the lock. That Madame, thinks Mammy, he gonna
git a dose o' licks.

It sounds as if at least three people have walked into
the flat.

That Boss-fella. Mammy says: 'Whyn't you tellum
leave you alone. Say you ain' up, Sugar,' Mammy says.

'I ain' up, Sugar,' calls out George as Valkyrie Frieda
strides into the room.

She is terribly upset to find her patient isn't ready,
and furthermore has what Dr Frieda designates as a
Furunkel on his podex. An illicit boil that has cropped
up only a fortnight after another boil had been dealt
with *definitively* by her distinguished colleague Docteur

Meyer who had subsequently refused to recognize the possibility of further trouble from this direction.

And now here is trouble with a rogue Furunkel suppurating, and Dr Frieda's English deserting her as usual in her hour of need.

'Georges! Why aren't you more advanced?'

Mr Crombie has to catch his plane in half an hour! She punts round setting the scene. 'Und also, why has this Furunkel not forthwith been notified? I am most pained, and Docteur Meyer will be also extremely output when he hears about it.'

Life is not being kind to Dr Frieda who, apart from a laudable wish always to have any patient of hers in a permanent state of readiness for every contingency, is especially keen in the case of this Australian surgeon, this fourth opinion expressly called in by M. Armand Benoir for whom Dr Frieda has a strong weakness.

This Schwärmerei is clamouring for a clean white coat to replace the still immaculate overalls she is wearing, and for a quick run over the jaw and upper lip with a dry shaver.

Now none of this can take place simply and solely because the patient's nurse, a coloured woman, has failed in her duty to prepare him, and because the patient himself has further aggravated the delay with his verfluchter Furunkel.

'This is no time for baths!' barks Dr Frieda, acutely aware that now she will have to appear before her Prinz unshaven and unshorn. 'Prepare the bed, please, Mme Madeleine. Make quickly, please. I am expecting Mr Crombie in exactly three minutes!'

She herself will attend to George's boil. She asserts

plaintively, 'I am still not able to comprehend, Mme Madeleine, why you are not more frontwards with the patient's disrobing?'

This is sheer mismanagement! Dr Frieda exhorts:

'For the want of a nail the horse was lost,
For the want of a horse the rider was lost,
For the want of a rider the battle was lost –
Und all for the want of a horseschuhnail!

So you see, little Georges, what a bad thing is unpre-paredness und how it could lose our battles for us, would we but let it!'

This homily is received in complete silence by George and Mammy as part of their anti Boss-Hart policy. The fact that she's dealing with a painful boil gently and expertly cuts no ice with them at all.

They have long ago made up their minds to hate her and have no intention of relinquishing, even for a moment, what over the months has grown into a favourite sport. Boss-Hart Watching is the one attraction the Clinic holds for them both. Every move of hers is followed by their inscrutable eyes. For them she is the Missing Link.

Now as she expatiates on Pünktclichkeit she can feel their relentless gaze on her, taking it all in. Her sang de boeuf complexion, her doggy smile, the flecks of foam collecting at the corners of her mouth, and, most rewarding of all, that blue and burglarish shadow now stealthily creeping over her face in the bright August sun.

10

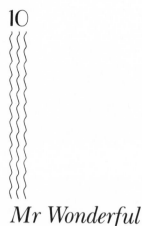

Mr Wonderful

'You have a very, very unique view here, by gollies, have you ever!' exclaims Keith Crombie. His thick, grey curls are felted against his flushed and corpulent neck. He could do with a beer.

He's a blowby from Australia where he has lately been hailed as 'Mr Wonderful' by the Melbourne press for his unconventional approach to his particular branch of surgery and the mounting score of near miracles attributed to his methods. Now he's having the landmarks of Paris pointed out to him from the pent-house floor of the Clinique Benoir by his distinguished French colleague, Fabien Courvoisier.

L'Opéra. Le Trocadéro. La Tour Eiffel.

'By G!' marvels Keith Crombie. He knows this professor Courvoisier. They met up last March at the Int. Soc. of Haematology Convention in New York. Not a likeable type, but unquestionably the foremost blood specialist in Europe today. Perhaps in the world. No doubt at all his use of combined drugs in the case of this

French bub has induced two marked remissions. According to the report sent out to him when the whole thing was being mooted, this second remission has already lasted for well over twelve weeks.

Question: Will it last long enough to attempt complete exchange transfusions?

Answer: At a glance, he'd say no.

Question: How strong are the relatives actually for an op?

Answer: With the exception of the English stepfather, he'd say not at all.

Even if he could quote them a fifty-fifty chance, he'd say not at all.

Bit of an awkward pozzy, could be. Aside from that he'd call the environment ideal. No worries at all about the Clinic. It's a beaut. One out of the box. So's the equipment. So's the quality of the nursing by what he's seen from his tour of the place this morning. Absolutely A okay plus. Good. Look at the bub first, iron the bugs out later. In any case he'll have to shoot off directly after the examination. He has this op at the Royal Children's, Melb, on the ninth, and he wants to rest up for at least a couple of days prior to. See his sisters, Verna and Darleen, maybe shoot off to Adelaide to see his brother Carl, though, as things are working out, he might have to give that one away. He'll have to stop over a day or two to see the thing right in Melb before flying back here to operate on Frenchie. If the family give him the old thumbs up, that is. If the op's a wrap he'll collect the girls and they'll put in a week's ski-ing in the Snowies. He'd like that. He feels tired. He could do with a real frosty beer.

'Paris is a very divine city, I'll tell you that!' declares Keith Crombie, who hasn't even been looking.

He walks into the flat where his hundred and four-teenth case of acute primary monocytic leukaemia is waiting for him, his eyes still filled with pictures of Carl and Darl and white Melbourne trams diving off Collins Street straight into the sunset.

'This the bub?' Keith Crombie proffers a thick veal cutlet of a hand. 'How are you, Georgie-boy?'

Golliwogs. Poor little bastard's going to shoot through.

'I'm good, thanks,' says Keith Crombie in answer to sincere enquiries from Dr Frieda. 'I hear the bub's not been too good lately? That right? Too bad. Have to change all that. Too right we will. Have you playing footie any minute now. And that's for sure,' promises Keith Crombie.

He tells Dr Frieda: 'Get the lass to open up those blinds, will you? Just a blink. That's the shot. Let's have some light on the subject.'

He's looking at the boil with clever little eyes. 'Gets a lot of these brutes, does he? What a scungy do. Not to worry. Everything's under control. She'll be right on the night,' says genial Keith Crombie from Australia. He takes his eyes off George's thigh. 'I think the chappie'd like a drink of water if the lass'ud getum one.'

Getum relaxed. The way it looks now there's a chance of him turning crook on the examination.

'By G. That looks good. What isut?' asks Crombie, who has never heard of capillaire, let alone seen it. His rabid thirst for ice-cold beer has come back worse than ever. Victoria Bitter. First thing he'll ask for when he boards his plane. Haven't a clue how to make beer over here. Lubra's pee, French beer.

He waits till George has finished his drink, then he says casually: 'Good'n'cyool, wasut? What about taking a look at things, Georgie?' Just a quick peek before he catches his plane.

'Ready when you are, doctor,' says Crombie. She is ready, too. So is the patient. Unless, of course, Mr Crombie would prefer a radical removal of the clothing?

He wags his great grey block. 'This'll do fine. Don't want the bub to catch cyold. Thanks a lot, doctor,' adds Crombie.

'You are most wilkomm,' says Dr Frieda, archly flashing her glasses. How much she is relishing that noble Beethoven-head. That red neck bright with manly sweat. Those sagacious pachyderm peepers.

Her Mr Wundervoll! He is not so dainty as her Prinz – this is true – but what a contrast between the heroic Crombie and the miserable Winkler and Zultz. (She summarily dispenses with the hyphen.) Swiss butterballs! thinks Dr Frieda witheringly of Walter Winkler and Dietrich Dieter-Zultz. Thanks God she is a German.

'Good-oh,' says Crombie as he examines his patient with hands that have earned him the world title Mr Wonderful and look like two hands of bananas.

It's all there for him to look at. One more case of acute leukaemia in a ten-year-old with all the usual sequelae from moon-faced pallor to sloughing areas of skin.

He's already had the full report, of course, with its history of bronchitis, pneumonia, blood in the urine, ulcers in the mouth and bowels, diarrhoea and difficulty in swallowing. A blue do, if ever. Well, that's it.

'All done,' says Crombie. Have to give that one away. The argument against an op is massive. Probably gain some slight improvement in the bub's condition. But at what cost? And for how long? Intensive injection techniques plus total sterility would entail cutting the bub off from his family for prolonged periods. Seeing his mother through a glass panel. Talking to her over a sterile phone.

He can't see it happening with Frenchie. From the report his whole temperament is against it; and his own doctor's verdict: 'an unsuitable subject', Crombie goes along with one hundred per cent.

He says cheerily: 'I expect the chappie'd like to go home now, if the lass would getum dressed?'

Nice lass, the bub's nurse. Doctor's a good lass, too. Too bad about the bub. 'Cheerio, blue,' he's holding out a genial bunch of fives. See himself out. Not to worry. Let you two girls get on withut.

From the door he says: 'Tell you one thing, Georgie. You have a very tremendous view up here. Very tremendous,' says Crombie, who hopes never to see that view again. 'Been nice knowing you,' says Crombie. 'Take good care now, and see you soon, Georgie. Georgie-Porgie,' says happy never-to-be-returning Keith Crombie from Australia.

11

Castleton v. the Sioux

His brother-in-law comes in with the announcement:
'Crombie has finished with us, Mi. We can all go home.'

'Hullo, that was quick.' Castleton gets up and joins
them. 'What did he say?'

'Who?'

'Crombie.'

'Nothing. What should he say?' asks Marguerite.

'Quite a lot actually.' Castleton flushes. 'What about
tests and things? Didn't he make any?'

Not to her knowledge. She turns to her brother who
has just come back from seeing Crombie to his taxi. 'Is
George nearly ready, Benoir?'

Yes, he is ready. Benoir says, smiling: 'Puss really has
his shirt tails flying this morning. He's coming home with
us.'

But what about Crombie? Castleton protests, 'I'd have
liked a word. I thought he was giving the kid a complete
overhaul in view of this operation.'

What operation? Marguerite points out no operation
has ever been in question so far as she is concerned.

Castleton asks flatly: 'Then what was the point of flying Crombie all the way from Australia?'

'No point at all,' replies his wife.

Benoir puts in quickly, 'An operation was envisaged some while back. . . .'

'Never by me,' says Marguerite.

'. . . when puss's general condition was more favourable.'

There is absolutely no question of any surgery now.

'Isn't there, now? Well, blow me down,' says Castleton.

'I am going to fetch moumou, Benoir,' says Marguerite. 'We shall be here forever if it's left to Madeleine to dress him.'

'Oy, 'arf a mo! *Mim!*' Castleton shouts after her. Too late. She's gone.

'What's up with *her*, then?' Castleton wants to know. He can feel himself starting to glow all over. A gassy smell like carbide fills his nose. Adrenalin, thinks Castleton, this is what adrenalin smells like. He feels about nine foot tall as well as scarlet in the face. He says in a loud voice: 'I've had your sister, Benoir, I've had her up to here.'

She has no normal standards that he can see. She certainly has no manners.

Actually, it was Benoir who had told him this first. Right at the outset of the marriage he had said, smiling: 'Don't even try to understand her, fella. When you've had enough just reach for your hat.'

Well, he's had it now, and he's getting out. 'And don't give me any crap about deserting Mim in her hour of need, because she couldn't need me less. Her behaviour of the past few weeks has made that *very* clear. Bloody Sioux,' says Castleton. 'I've had the lot of you.'

'All the same,' returns his brother-in-law, smiling, 'I hope you won't decide to leave us yet.'

He has stepped out on to the balcony and is standing at the balustrade, smoking and looking at Paris. When he comes in again he says: 'It's magnificent, that view. It never fails to astonish me. No one is trying to deceive you about puss, you know.'

Castleton says rudely: 'It looks jolly like it from where I'm standing. Crombie comes over to examine the kid. Stays five minutes and pisses off again without a blind word. Too bloody silly,' says Castleton.

Benoir says reasonably: 'It would take a little time to mount an examination like that.'

'Like what?'

'Any extensive examination.'

'Well, bugger that for a start.' He has heard some rubbish in his life, thinks Castleton, but this is yer actual.

Benoir reminds him: 'He has an operation to perform in Melbourne on the ninth, I believe.'

Well, bugger that as well. 'What does he take us for?' Castleton says. 'We fly him over and all he can think about is his bloody Australian operation. What did he say about *George*? He must have an opinion. He examined the kid,' says Castleton. 'Or didn't he?'

'No.'

'Why not?' He hates his brother-in-law suddenly and wholeheartedly.

As if he knows, Benoir answers stiffly: 'Crombie is in full agreement with the doctors over here.'

So that's it. Just because five quacks agree, that's to be it. 'All systems stop,' says Castleton.

'That is the thing in outline,' agrees Benoir.

But why? 'There are other doctors, you know. Crombie's isn't the only opinion worth having.'

All the same, Benoir thinks the opinion of the five foremost names in haematology might be worth considering.

So. No more treatment. Benoir says firmly: 'Everyone who loves puss is agreed on this. And, when you have thought about it, so will you be.'

Castleton says bitterly: 'No wonder you never let on which way you were voting.' So death is the only thing for the kid. Benoir is as good as telling him so. To prolong life as the thing stands, would have no meaning whatsoever. Let it end. Before he gets the hearing aid and calipers. He has the spectacles already.

Ah, yes. Well now. Seeing the kid in glasses. Castleton says brutally: 'That must be a blow for the Sioux.'

'That's right,' agrees Benoir. He has gone very pale. He lights a fresh cigarette and says: 'In any case, puss would never survive an operation, so why commit the final stupidity? I have seen it happen before and it would happen again in spite of giant strides forward in this field.'

He's talking about his mother, but Castleton can't bother about that. With a keen cast of doctors and surgeons he is devising monster programmes of bigger and better operations featuring injections, splenectomies, blood transfusions, and introducing a novelty. Impacts with laser rays.

Benoir begins to laugh.

'What's funny?'

'You are funny,' returns his brother-in-law. 'You love puss so much you want to unleash all these horrors on him.'

Anything's better than this Vichy defeatist attitude of his and Marguerite's. If no further steps were going to be taken what the hell was the use of calling in Crombie?

'I think it must have been to please you,' Benoir says. He adds as casually as if he were mentioning a cancelled engagement: 'I'm afraid puss isn't going to be able to make it, Vince.'

'Not make it?'

No. Courvoisier has given him three months. 'Top,' says Benoir.

Castleton stares at him aghast.

'Top,' says Benoir.

'I don't believe it.' He hates his brother-in-law more than ever.

Benoir shrugs, but Castleton heckles him. 'You think it's bloody hopeless, don't you? You think he's going to die. Well, I don't think so. I don't believe it. Not at all.' He's making a horrible din.

'His mother has accepted it,' is all Benoir will say. At the door he adds, formally: 'If I could exchange my life for his I would do it.'

'I'm sure,' says Castleton, vulgarly. In the middle of it all Marguerite sweeps in, demanding: 'What is going on in here? What is the shouting about?' She tells her brother: 'I have sent George home. Mammy can put him to bed before lunch.'

She is staring at Castleton as if he were a stranger.

'I have put it to Vince about puss, Mi. Quite naturally he is upset.'

'Upset! What's that supposed to mean?' asks Castleton. 'Can't you say anything without beating about the bush? Mealy-mouthed blighter!'

'What is he talking about, this maniac?' demands Marguerite. She turns on Castleton and says in furious tones:

'Don't dare to speak to my brother in that disgusting fashion. My brother has shown you consideration beyond the point of reason and you are behaving like the biggest boor.'

'Oh, do shut up about your brother, girl,' Castleton says. 'If he's your lover, that's another thing.'

There is a silence.

'You have understood nothing about this whole business,' Marguerite tells him. 'Absolutely nothing at all.'

Chance is a fine thing. Castleton says: 'I'm never told anything. I'm never consulted. I just toe the line with the rest of the staff and wait for the next bulletin.'

'Since you put it like that,' says Marguerite.

'Let it rest, Mi,' says her brother, but she goes right up to Castleton and tells him to his face: 'Don't try to give your orders here, my friend. Ever since we came to Paris you have been throwing your weight about over my son. If you want to know the truth you are making moumou unhappy with your interference. You are incapable of minding your own business. Are you coming, Armand, or are you staying in this madhouse?' asks Marguerite.

No, he is coming with her. Since it is pointless to remain. They leave the unseemly room together, shutting the door on the unspeakable Castleton, the spectacle of his misery and loud abusive rage.

They are only going home to lunch, but Castleton thinks furiously: She's going off with Benoir again.

Ever since this latest phase of the kid's illness, she's made no secret of the fact that Benoir comes to her bed.

'We try to get a little sleep together, is that so bad?'

It's so bad, suddenly, all of it, that he bursts into tears.

12

The Gropers and the Schnappers

On August 4, after lunch, while George is resting, a one comes along who asks him to come for a walk.

George doesn't answer, so the one, who looks like Mr Viv but isn't, starts walking. George can see him farther up the road listening and waiting for him to come up.

The one starts to talk. His voice smells horribly of half-digested food and wine. Of fish and blood and a sweet custardy smell that is the worst of all.

His hands are fingerless and hard, like heavy oars.

They walk along the railway lines where rayless camomile is growing and blowing in the wind from the trains, past the marshalling yards towards the ink-blue tarn.

There is a grab at work here, yawning and grabbing and twisting about in mid-air like an animal.

The noise from the tarn is deafening and cancels the noise from the crane. It's quite full of sharks and crocodiles, crashing and barging about in the water only half submerged, with blazing eyes and open jaws like pianos with the lids up.

The water is also crowded with fish which are climbing over each other's backs to escape the banging lids.

Hideous fish with hideous names, like blueface and
flathead and gropers and schnappers, their stale eyes red
and sunken with the effort of trying to save themselves.

O no! screams George. The one is laughing com-
posedly behind his oar.

A train shoots shrieking out of the marshalling yard
and straight through the tarn and into a fold in the
hills and instantly all the miserable fish fall to the bottom
of the tarn and are seen no more.

In the silence the whining of the crane starts up again.

The one is now pointing upwards with his oar to where
the devil's house is standing on the bluff, a high-
shouldered brush bathing-hut on stilts overlooking the
now silent tarn. The one now grabs his hand, and they
make up the steep incline together, scrambling and
slipping up the forest floor, metallic with fir mast like
steel filings.

The woods around here are peopled with ghosts. Here
the Stoneheads are charging through the undergrowth,
axing the fern with their stone axes, and there are many
snakes like snow white ropes amongst the fern.

They pass Revenants in their hobble skirts, and square
ghosts like hat boxes, rollicking three and four abreast.
Last of all come the dark rotund bodies of flaming
ghosts. Some are already roasted brown, others still
flaming like gyrating Christmas puddings. These last are
setting fire to everything they pass.

The pandemonium raised by the passing ghosts is like
a carnival, but at the devil's house all is silent, and at
the door a stained-looking may tree is making a difficult

second blooming, the pink bleeding weakly into the white.

'It will come red,' says the devil, who is also Mr Viv. Both are nodding. The hut is terribly hot. George feels very bad so they give him some water to drink while he stands outside.

The water is very good. It's so cold it's almost sweet. He still feels terribly bad. There is a row of dead dogs lying outside, draining into the gutter. They all have their leads and collars on but most of them are without their heads. George tries not to look in case he should see the little dog of his Tante Marie among them, but Mr Viv is lifting all the bodies up with his pointy shoes and letting them flop back again.

He catches sight of Ouistiti, still alive. He's huddled into a corner wringing his hands and crying in French for Uncle Benoir.

O no! O no! He calls out so loud that they give him the water again. The water fills him like a vase. It doesn't only go into his stomach. It fills every part of him with a sweet ache. His shoulders are full of cold water. He feels better. The ground where the dogs were lying is all cleared up, and there's nothing to see now but a withered field.

This is the field he has heard about. The field of Leukaemia and Allied Diseases of the Blood. He doesn't want to live here, he wants to go home, but as he turns to go he sees the meek may tree at the door is all white again and he is lying in the field in his freezing raspberry-ice vomit.

13

Magic Time

The Bienvilles are lying in bed at their honeymoon hotel, the legendary Pélerinage at Eden Roc. They are drinking Scotch and discussing their new three-level penthouse overlooking the Bois which he has just bought and she is currently decorating.

Bienville's young wife, Elaine, has just got back from a flying visit to Paris to check on progress with their architect. She is in transports over the new apartment.

'So what went right?' Bienville wants to know.

Everything. She loves him.

It's what he needs. 'When did it happen?' asks Bienville.

She has loved him from the beginning, and she will love him to the end.

He considers this outlook pretty unattractive, and says so.

She starts some boring thing about her brother still being in love with his wife – big deal – 'after two-and-a-half years of married life'.

'Your brother is a swish,' says Bienville, 'so love don't mean a thing to him except easy dough.'

Added to which, his Frau is in dried bananas or something hideous, so he loves her to the maximum. She is 'Bananes Zoum', says Bienville, 'le meilleur déjeuner pour les gosses.'

It is not true!

It isn't true? He is stupefied, 'You mean she is *not* "Bananes Zoum" le meilleur déjeuner pour les gosses?'

She is. But that is not the reason why he loves her. 'You'll see for yourself,' predicts Elaine.

What will he see? And when will he see it?

'When they join us on our vacation in Spain.'

'Over my dead ass,' says Bienville.

'Oh, Fred, you aren't chic!' complains Elaine, who thinks it smart and English to call her husband Fred. 'Why are you always horrible about my family?'

'My *deah,* you're goin' on a bit, my deah,' Bienville reminds her. He has a British Fortnight on, so for the past two weeks people have either been *going* on or *carrying* on.

Before that they'd had a Speak German week, but the effect upon his Vater had been so kolossal that Bienville had been obliged to scrub around the Schweinerei for Angst his Vater would platz into eine Million Stücke und so weiter.

'Ich liebe mein Vater,' declares Bienville.

How she hates him when he talks like that! Elaine bursts out: 'I don't understand a single word of that horrible language!'

'It's great when you're gifted,' agrees Bienville.

In any case since when has it been okay for the French to fraternize with the Germans?

He tells her. Since the late war when the de Greniers won a gold for collaboration.

Oh, no. It's too much. She bursts into tears. It's the same thing every time she gets back from Paris. She was so happy about the new apartment. 'I wanted to tell you all about it and now you are in a filthy mood.'

He remains quiet and even smiling. As usual she has no clue to what he is thinking. 'What is the matter? Has something happened, Fred?'

'My papa doesn't love me,' is the strange reply, 'but you can run into my arms any time, because I love you, baby.'

'Oh, Fred!' She thought he was talking to her, so she's stopped crying. She's even wiped her rabbity nose, though it's still twitching pinkly. So now his idiot wife is giving him wet kisses because his idiot wife never will learn.

'Oh, Fred, I wish you would come to Paris with me and see it! The progress is fantastic!' She swears to him he wouldn't recognize it from a week ago, the progress has been so fantastic!

Felicidads.

Everything about the new apartment is fabulous and fantastic. She's out of her shoes about the new apartment. Colour TV in every room. Piped music. Service escalators.

Service escalators? 'Baby, you should of said,' says Bienville. He's *really* with her now. He bought this place blind in order to catch the full impact of the de Grenier blueprint for a home, and here it's paying off already.

Also, it is to be his great revenge on Herman the German. He's sick to his tripes of Benoir and his high-class shines. Now everything's turning out better than funny. It's Magic Time! So, as soon as his idiot wife reports the heated pool on the patio with the Op-Art surround, 'Lady, I *hafta* know!' cries Bienville.

This dame is really making it for me, thinks Bienville when he learns that the entrance hall has a terrace with massive main bedroom suites, plus the servants' quarters on the same level!

'Above this. . . .'

'Hey, what's above this?' Bienville instantly wants to know. 'C'*mawn*! I hafta know! What's this above this business?'

A wrap-around terrace. Elaine adds casually: 'It's the latest thing in the States, you know.'

'Wrap-around? Terrace? Jeez!' marvels Bienville, exulting progressively as each fresh glory is presented to him.

A wrap-around terrace with morning, dining- and drawing-rooms! '*With* lift,' amends Elaine. Also a service gallery. '*With* service lift,' amends Elaine.

'*Another lift?* We get *two* lifts? And all for peanuts,' crows Bienville, who by now is practically falling out of bed. She is ecstatic, too, about their thrilling new apartment. She has never seen anything like it in her life. But also as much because, this time, if only momentarily, she has managed to lift the obsessional gloom over his cousin's illness Fred seems unable to shake off.

Till now he has always refused to accompany her to Paris, or to take any interest in suggestions for further improvements their architect still sends them from time to time. But tonight, thanks to her great effort, he suddenly can't hear enough about their flat.

It seems that the whole top floor of this super tepee is occupied by an absolutely *vast roof-garden* with – wait for it – *full-sized trees*! A cinema with projection chamber, a library, a studio, and a Vegas-type rumpusroom stuffed with one-arm bandits!

'What happened to the moat? I gotta *know*! Tell, tell!' beseeches Bienville.

Finally, there is *another* gallery, a kind of a voyeur's dream, which actually looks down on to the entire living area!

'Baby, you *bury* me!' moans Bienville.

'Oh, Fred, it's fabulous! It's the most glamorous apartment in Paris. And what an investment! Listen, in two years it'll be worth five times the price you gave for it!' She is in transports of de Grenier delight. Especially about the investment. Her eyes are quite circular with pleasure. She's far too excited to notice the look on her husband's face.

For *dreck*, he is thinking, this venue leaves even that Versailles-sized Normandy Chaumière-type residence of the de Greniers standing (right where it is, at La Baule). This venue is *all* dreck, and going from strength to strength as Elaine and her butch fairy of a Yank interior decorator get into their stride. This fruit is minty as hell, and everything he lays his mitts on bears his mark. Even his name's beyond expectations. Ozzie Fuerst!

Now the thing *is*: You could practically build and fully equip one of those clinics Hermie is kinky for with the wampam just that revolving sun-deck is going to take by the time Fuerst Ozzie is all through dreaming up the

ultimate in Odeon-type air conditioning. And this is
seriously valuable, because, in Bienville's view, Herman
the German has been getting more and more uppity of
late, and has now come to the climax.

So here is Mr Viv getting together his great, big, beautiful Drekpalast for the sole purpose of taking Herman
down a peg.

He has the scene set up. A house-warming party for
two hundred guests, to include his alcoholic in-laws.
Separate tables lit from below. The full nite-spot treatment. Drugstore-type eats and over-iced champagne.
Piped music. At his table he'll bring the conversation
round to li'l Marie, his sufferings, his cute sayings, and
immediately the alcoholic in-laws will start singing his
praises to the sound of sawn-off violins.

But, just as Herman gropes, gagging, for the exits,
bam! They are letting down this giant screen already,
and on this screen, in technicolour and full-dimensional
sound, is the feature-length movie of the Benoir-de
Grenier wedding.

How vulgaire, commun, ordinaire, de mauvais goût et
banal can you get?

That Benoir. He has it promised. Beaucoup popola
this time, Benoir, thinks Bienville.

'Benoir is scat!' is going to be Bienville's new slogan.
He wakes his wife to tell her.

'Oh, Fred, I was *asleep*!' exclaims the nutter. As the
last thing he wants is more dialogue with her about the
new flat, he orders her to dress. 'C'mon. I wanna dance.
Mush!' calls out Bienville.

14

Conversation in Progress

There is a gentle click.

Bienville shouts furiously: 'I think you ought to know your name equates with shit.' There is no reply. But there's a chance he's still on the line, so Bienville calls out loudly: 'So that's in case you think nobody's smelled it.'

Which is just about everything he has to say. Except: 'Oh yeah, big kiss to my cousin the Naegeli Type.'

Shot down! But the superior silence is already turning the childish victory sour.

'That Auteuil is *nowhere*,' thinks Bienville, hanging up. 'I mean it is a nowhere place.' He has never felt so angry in his life. What the hell is the matter with Hermie these days? He must've suddenly got it through his hat that Thingo is worse, so he has to make a big production number of everything.

Just now he's out of his tree about Bienville not showing at that so famous *lit de douleur* every hour on the hour of every day. The current kick-up has been hideous beyond belief.

'You have sunk to the lowest level of behaviour, Bien-ville,' has been elected the running gag.

Things had been different back in the early days when they'd spent hours fun-talking over the instrument. Some-times two and three times a day.

Nap at his flirtatious best, enquiring after *la jeune ménage*, expecting Boucher-like doings with the young couple sulking and making up amidst the rumpled bed-clothes, the roses, the cage-birds and chamber pots that appeal most to his rococo eroticism.

Tante once told him that the pretty mister has a special thing about fine bed linen.

He had entertained Hermie lavishly with news of the honeymoon. Also a serialized version of the de Grenier Saga, a *roman policier* Hermie adores, about the doings of his alcoholic in-laws, with Elaine's mother (keep away from naked lights) and a terrible aunt by marriage in a terrible mink coat (Bienville has recently invested her with a chain of bordellos right across metropolitan France) as chief characters. The Aunt has a hideaway on Dunk Island, which is just off Marseilles, where she owns a heroin factory.

For one of these instalments, Hermie will swop you the latest from Neuilly. Classics, like this last idea of Punkie Castleton's for a cure for Thingo.

'This time it's surgical,' says Benoir, who's giggling so much he can hardly speak.

It seems that this time the Punk is gunning for Thingo's spleen.

This is the most to date. So?

Complete removal is the answer. Nothing less. Benoir says calmly: 'He loves puss very much.'

'Sounds like it!'

Unhappily it's a fact.

On the lighter side there is a Mr Wonderful. An Australian surgeon who specializes in this operation. He has been highly recommended by the Punk's bro, who is a British naval Punk with wall-to-wall humanity. Bienville has seen him at Tante's wedding, a dainty father figure in old Spanish lace.

'Don't tell me you're having this Abo look Marie over?' Bienville calls out.

Most certainly. He has already been. He was expected on the first of August.

So what happened?

Nothing. There was another consultation. This time with five doctors instead of four. Nobody wanted to operate, so puss kept his *tripes* intact.

'Vince had a touching faith in me,' confides the pretty Fixer. 'I'm afraid a little got lost.'

Hermie is gorgeous. Out of sight. He's the lookingest and the onliest and his son adores him. Imprudent Bienville calls out: 'How's Marie making out these days?'

Wham! Typically and without warning Benoir is suddenly acting seamy as hell. His cousin is far from well. In case Bienville has forgotten, he has a case of Moncytic Leukaemia of the Naegeli type.

'Get the hell over tomorrow, hear me? Get that lead out of your pants.'

To which he had instantly replied: 'Tomorrow we have to be in Dublin to look at horses. I'm on my honeymoon, Papa.'

There is a pause before the pleasant voice enquires:

'How come you can never be more than all right, Bienville?'

And after that the gentle click.

Tampata. Incommunicado. I've cooled on *you* boy,
thinks Bienville.

15

Flak

They have got back from something draggy and Bienville is trying to get the Ritz again.

There is still a lot of flak.

' 'Allo! Qu'est-ce que se passe? And what the hell goes *on*?' Bienville seems to be calling out to no one in particular. This is 3 a.m. so his wife is you betcha, as well, calling out: 'Why don't you leave it? You have already tried twice without success to contact them. I find your family simply extraordinary. Surely if anything happened to your *poor* cousin they would have let you know at once?'

'Skip the buzz,' is Bienville's advice.

Apparently they are still burning his effigy over at the Ritz, because again they are for ever putting him through.

Bienville decides if, when he calls again, Benoir still nixes on speaking to him, then he'd forget about calling for a week or two.

After this last non-comeback he has no notion of playing Mista Milktoast to any of them.

Meanwhile there are signs of his being put through.

'Papa?'

' 'Allo?'

It's that feeb sec. of Nap's again. 'Bonsoir, Monsieur Bienville.'

'Bonsoir my ass and likewise my reproductive organ – and also, and on the side, I desire to speak to my father.'

The fancy pansy instantly fears this will not be possible.

'Goof off,' says Bienville.

The feeb goofs off and back again. The griffe remains the same. Monsieur is not available. Reason: Monsieur is in the room of Monsieur Bienville's cousin.

'And my mother?'

Mme Benoir is also there.

Quel dommage. So howzabout Bienville talkin' to Missus Castleton? 'A miniscule get-together dahlin'. Would that be nice?'

The feeb regrets but Mrs Castleton is also, too, and what is more *as well*, in that very identical room.

In that case Bienville suggests a matey word with Mista Cee. 'Know who I mean? Nunc the Punk. Walks on his knuckles. Sock him over, doll,' Bienville says. 'I'm in the mood.'

It's wild. It's out of sight. But the Punk's in there *as well*! In fact it's where they all are *at*, the fag is telling him. Medics, nurses, housemaids, valets, chauffeurs, chefs, sous-chefs, plongeurs and especially plongeurs' second cousins.

All, all, this sickening fag reports, are in the room of Monsieur Bienville's cousin.

'So what is he using for air?' asks Bienville, hanging up. And that is in case they are by any chance thinking he is the world's Original Decorated Mug.

16

The Roses, the Lilacs,
the Eucharist Lilies

Great firm, the Sioux. Branches throughout the civilized world.

And, anyways, will someone please tell him what the hell *good* would it do for him to go home? The last time it had been Panic City, with all the blacks making musk up in Marie's room. And when you'd climbed through that and finally made the bed, there are the French and the British all mad for involvement in the Puss Benoir Experience.

A favourite duet of his father's and Tante's has now been orchestrated for him under the able baton of Hermie. He's late. His cousin has been expecting him since breakfast/lunch/dinner. How is it he can never be on time?

'We panned at Nîmes, Papa, and had to change a shoe,' says Bienville, kissing his father affectionately. In spite of everything, it's splendid to be home.

'Bonsoir, Maman. Bonsoir, Tantan Mi.'

His mother and aunt are splendid, too. Their perfume

wrecks the room. Only the pretty mister means him no good. He starts to rough it up.

'At Nîmes! You must be out of your skull to come by road. And you excuse yourself by saying you burst a tyre. Next time you either fly or stop away,' snarls Nap, rolling his celebrated eyes.

'Okay, I fly,' says Bienville in a fairly patient voice. He tries to take his father's arm, but Nap is still studying war.

'Back off me, hear me? Try to behave for once. And for the future, fly or keep away. I won't give you a second time.'

'Okay, I said okay.' He is here at the bed, where everything's white. The sheets. The deathfest flowers. Those roses and lilacs and eucharist lilies. But Thingo, that show-off, he has to be the whitest of all.

A dew of sweat has broken out on Bienville's lip.

He's cashing his chips under their very noses. Putting the shuck on them all. Man, he could howl like a dog. Nap is demanding: 'What are you staring at?' and 'Aren't you going to kiss your cousin?'

'Hi, Typhoid,' Bienville says, flipping a wrist. There is nothing to be seen but a head on a pillow. No hands, no neck, no anything but this John the Baptist head. Man, when he looks at that head he could just die alive. He stands there, hoping to get off, but Nap is giving the go-ahead.

'What are you waiting for, Bienville?'

'Hi.' He is afraid the lips are cold or that the breath will smell. He bends and kisses his cousin's face. The cheeks are cold, the lips are cold, and the cold breath smells.

'Hi, Uglybug,' says Bienville, almost normally. Everyone is handing out prohibitions in depth. It is, for example, extremely défense de fumer. His father says quite kindly: 'Put it out, fella. Puss's eyes tear so.' But the Punk is really running at the mouth about it.

'No smoking, *Purleese*,' this sassy Briton is exclaiming, while a French Fuss is in progress as to whether or not you are one-hundredth of a millimetre too near that poachy bed in which the head now spends its maximum security life.

Too bad the goodniks don't know he could yet have himself a time in bed with the head at warehouse prices. Yes *sir*. The head has opened one eye and is smiling at him with it.

17

The Laff-Lab

This room is hell. I wish I was outa this laugh laboratory, Bienville thinks.

'Hiya, Typhoid,' Bienville says again.

'Let it end, Viv,' advises Benoir.

'But Papa, I'm dating,' Bienville protests. He has broken out all over with sweat again. 'You, Typhoid, you payin' me some mind?'

'My face is cold,' announces the head. The eye closes but the smile remains.

'Hey, will ya look at me?' Bienville calls out. 'Listen, you figuring on going to that kooky wood again? Know where I mean, that camp park?'

'Viv, I said end it.'

'But Papa, I'm dating, I swear it. I hafta see that park, don't I? I gotta see those dumdum flowers Marie was telling about.'

The head nods silently, once.

'See what I mean?' This place was a park or some-wheres his cousin had got taken to every day before he turned into a head. Probably the Monceau.

'I bet they're beautiful, those dumdum flowers,' cries Bienville, affectedly tipping his wrist. 'I bet they're just so beautiful.'

He embarks on a lifelike impersonation of the Dauphin shortsightedly botanizing in this crazy park, kissing the soil of la belle France, sniffing at flowers and getting dog turds every time.

'O, it is only from dear little toutous, don't you know?' shrieks Bienville in his cousin's voice. 'We have all got to crap, don't you know, and we should not despise them for it.'

It's highly hilarious and everyone is laughing, even the Punk. Only Nap is still studying war. 'Use your respect when you talk to your cousin, hear me? Or take yourself off.'

Which is immediately cordial, and places Nap firmly, in Bienville's view, as première denizen of Rave City.

Dinner is announced. That is, some nigra glides into the room and out again without having uttered a word. Benoir enquires coldly: 'Are you dining with us or what?' Which is practically telling you you can hit the road at your own chosen speed.

Everyone is preparing to go down to dinner. Only Baldy-locks remains, presumably on the premise that the head will draw comfort from, and benefit by, his creepy British virtues. The head itself, after yawning luxuriously, has disappeared under the sheets. It is all excessively non-reassuring. Bienville asks nervously: 'Is Marie eating up here?'

'Puss eats with us,' is the calm reply, 'and if you ever came here you would know it.'

J. Christ! It's factual. Out of the corner of one eye

he has just seen a medic and two sisters slip into the room. Oh, horrors! They are going to dig Thingo out of bed and dude him up so he'll look sharp at table!

Hold my hand *purlees*! thinks Bienville, and beats it to the bathroom.

When he comes back they're still at it. Literally, all of them, with Hermie praising Thingo to the skies for even attempting to do up a button. As well as taking light years to accomplish, this is giving Thingo the kind of shakes that would be envied by the Mayor of Jell-O City.

Bienville is grateful to his aunt, who after two seconds is all through with the whole transaction, and saying briskly: 'My God, Benoir, let someone do it for him and permit us to go down to dinner in peace. In case George thinks he will make himself important by attempting to do up his sleeve! Give the sister your cuff and be quick about it!'

Tante is splendid! She is the Colosseum and Bienville loves her to death. Even now Interpol has driven Tante's talents underground, she can still turn the heat on for li'l Marie. Of course you have to catch her at it, and then it's not always the real stuff. Being policed by Nap and Nunc the Punk have driven Tante's splendid natural talents underground. Bienville remembers her as a brilliant exponent of l'Ecole Benoir, frequently breaking her own records.

Last summer, New Orleans, Bienville figures had been Tante's classic period. Happy times. It's an hélas they had to stop leaving the title virtually vacant.

They're going to eat. 'C'mawn, let's *go*!' cries Bienville, glad to be leaving the laff-lab to Baldy-locks and the living dead.

They are to meet in what Bienville thinks of as the wagon from the Morgue, a kind of electric trolley with Thingo on it, in the dining-room, but for the moment it's divine just to be going down in the lift with his mother and aunt, an arm around each of them.

Benoir he can ignore because, for Bienville's money, Benoir has been acting like a case of yaws for far too long.

When they get to the dining-room the party from the Morgue has already arrived. It's quite a crowd, comprising Thingo and the Punk, plus a medic plus a medic engineer, but Bienville contrives to keep his eyes off all of them while they decant Thingo from his trolley to his chair.

There is to be something splendid à l'ananas for dessert, and the heavy armoured fruit has already been lined up on a side table. Looky looky. Bienville manages to concentrate on that.

At table Benoir is letting the good times roll. He is going a storm with Maman and Thingo and Ouistiti, for all of whom he is a must. His very presence secures their happiness and Thingo has already fallen asleep twice on the table on account of he is so relaxed. There is no hurry music ever at the Ritz. Everything works for Benoir. Benoir is divine. So are his dinners, so is his gall, and there are times when his son would admire to kick him in the teeth. Like now for instance when he is announcing to the table at large: 'Puss is going on the town tomorrow. Viv's going to take him someplace nice.'

'What else is news around here?' Bienville wants to know. But Nap is making like he hasn't heard.

'Shall you like that, baby? Want Mr Viv should take you to a movie?'

'Like when for instance?' Bienville wants to know.

'Like tomorrow. Be here,' snaps Nap.

'Just when am I doing all this?' Bienville asks. He is genuinely trying to see himself. 'Honestly, Papa, I can't make it. Have a heart. I'm on my honeymoon.'

'Soit. Terminé,' says Benoir.

J. Christ. So now he has been nominated Leper of the Year. Bienville has to allow the pretty mister is at his cutest when he is mad, sitting there laughing and eating his peach and letting the smoke out through his pretty clenched teeth.

But only as long as the others are there. The instant Maman has gone to bed and Thingo has been carted off on his trolley and Punkie and Tante are up in the laff-lab with him saying good night, the good times are over and Hermie reverts to type.

'You have sunk to the lowest level of humanity,' snarls Hermie, whose milk of human whatsit has frozen solid in two seconds flat. 'It's clear that you have no thought for anything but your own pleasures, and that the plight of your cousin touches you not at all.'

He has said every word of this in French because, of course, Hermie is about as classy as you will ever get.

Bienville says mildly: 'I told you how it was with me. I'm on my honeymoon. I can't keep breaking it to visit with Marie all of the time. I'm sorry, Papa,' Bienville says.

'I am not interested in your excuses. Which are all phoney, by the way.'

Bienville makes no reply, but Hermie hasn't done with him yet. He has a big finish coming. 'Be sorry later,' Hermie says. 'Know how I mean?'

Chreeist. He's surprising himself by keeping his cool on account of he's always figured you have to make allowances for Benoir. You have to remember that for many years he was prize pupil at the dread Ecole Benoir which in itself, in Bienville's view, shows main-line talent because, of course, as pépère's personal bundle of joy, he'd learnt it all the hard way. Result, that switched on little rooster, Hermie as he is today, scratching and scratching and standing aside to let his hens and chickens peck up all the corn.

Bienville adores contes about pépère, who was exactly the kind of Spitzbub Bienville understands, and anything about Hermie's early life with him his son finds wholly fascinating.

It appears before Tante and Beau had stolen his scene, beautiful, bouncing Hermie had been the apple of the Spitzbub's terrible eye, and a favourite conte from that time has it that Hermie had frequently been displayed as a centre piece on the Spitzbub's sassy supper tables. An infant Sun-King naked for all to admire. Wow! Gurgling and crowing among the muscat grapes and nectarines.

Bienville asks good-naturedly : 'Hey, Papa, I ever tell you I bought me this peach of a fifteen-month-old at Chantilly? I tell you that fella's gonna make me a whole heap of bread. Right now with the flat I can use it,' confides Bienville, whose personal income is adequate to start up World War Three.

Bienville declares : 'You'll like him, Papa. He's colossal,' but Nap just looks at him and lets some more smoke out. It really fazes Bienville that Nap has this one-track mind.

He can't resist it. He observes: 'He has this kind of a grey hide, don't you know? Those big black eyes? I'd say the perfect monocytic type.' Bienville says: 'I guess I'll call him li'l Marie.'

The effect of this speech upon Nap is positively electrifying. He is completely out of his tree. For an instant it looks as if his eyes have turned a bright venomous brown. He says in a low voice: 'Take yourself off. Nobody needs you here.'

The Royal Razz. Which is just what Bienville has been waiting for. All he knows now is if Marie were to die tonight he wouldn't take one step in this direction.

'Excuse my dust,' says Bienville, and walks out of the house.

18

Fred

'Shut down. Froze solid,' announces Bienville, rejoining his wife who is doing her nails with silver paint to make them look like guitar pickers and anyhow thinks he is talking about the weather.

'The Ritz,' says Bienville in a loud voice, 'the Ritz is finally off the air.' The nut he is married to goes on electroplating her nails. They are much too small. He hates her minimouse nails. He also hates her hair which has been dyed grey to match her eyes. Or could be it is her eyes that have been dyed. If he ever knew which he has forgotten. In any case it is positively the least of his worries.

Three years at an English finishing school have fixed it so it is practically useless to tell her anything, but he can't stop himself talking about it. That Benoir is an Art form, Bienville decides. The way he has mounted this whole boycott-by-telephone thing.

Three days. Three days since Nap last uttered. It is very, very hilarious.

'Perhaps your father is busy,' gives out the nut, who knows scat-all about it. She is still shlocking the gunge around.

She reports excitedly: 'He was on TV again this afternoon. I had no idea your father was in politics, Fred. He looks fantastically young on the screen. I would like to see him again,' declares the nutter, very impressed. She is running at the mouth about how amusing everything was.

'Your father was smoking the whole time. I don't know what he was speaking about. My sister Gisèle was here from Cannes. She wanted to tell me about her engagement so we had the sound off, but it must have been amusing because your father was smiling nearly all the time.'

She asks him curiously: 'What does your father talk about on television, Fred?'

He talks about monocytic leukaemia of the Naegeli type.

'Really?'

'It makes him laugh a lot.'

As he's expected, she doesn't take it in. This lady, decides Bienville, knows *less* about any given thing. He drops down on the bed beside her and shoots out a small tan hand.

'C'mere. I wanna make love.'

It's the one thing he ever says she understands, but of course she has to turn the style on about it with typical de Grenier tastelessness.

Perhaps they shouldn't 'do it' while 'things' are so uncertain.

They could be called to Paris any moment.

He tells her briefly to shut up. It's a gas how loyal she has suddenly become vis-à-vis her former enemy now her little ally, who is doing her such a splendid turn by dying.

It's not true! Elaine protests: 'I've nothing against your poor cousin! How could one feel anything but pity for a child who is suffering like that?' *Except* he happens to *know*, she'd like to see Thingo in the chair and that it would give her enormous pleasure to personally throw the switch. 'Ever since you've known Marie you've smeared him. How come you're suddenly in the middle, lady?'

It isn't true! It isn't true!

Big production number?

Elaine protests: 'How can you say a thing like that? I simply can't understand you!'

And he can't understand this whole conversation.

'On the feet. I wanna make love.'

It's the worst hell to get her on to her feet. She's lobbying for a kiss but he ignores it. Actually he's listening for the phone.

'C'mon. Hold still. C'mon.'

He is supposed to be getting her out of this kind of an anti-dress which is intended to vavavoo you on account of it has only one fastening somewhere around the *navel*, and leaves – would you believe? – the *charlies* free and swinging, inside, but mostly outside, this kind of an anti-blouse.

For a thing like this, he is told, you actually pay good cash-money.

'D'you like it, Fred?'

He likes the farded nipples and give them his modified

support, but strictly, at the moment, he is bored by everything but listening for the phone.

He doesn't want to go to bed, so they do it as they are in a big chair. It's a bit dirty but quite good. Afterwards she says 'I love you' a lot, which can be boring. It's a disc she's taken to playing non-stop lately. A and B sides. The B side is called 'Do you love *me*?'

Incidentally, No. 1 track with his family these days is entitled 'When are you coming home?'

It's the now thing with the Sioux to act as if they alone are suffering while he is having himself a great big beautiful ball far from that so celebrated bed from which his cousin conducts his case of monocytic leukaemia.

Suddenly he wants more than anything to go home. In under five minutes he has everything organized and he and Elaine are hot-tailing it for the Ritz.

19

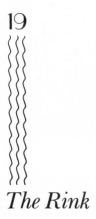

The Rink

'Where d'yo think you're going? *If* I may make so. bold,' adds Castleton in a loud voice. He's still asleep while he's saying it, the meaning fading as he wakes. He must have been dreaming Mim was leaving him to go to Benoir's bed again.

Lately this has been happening a lot. So has the dream. She probably only goes to get the comfort she doesn't want from him. As she'd be the first to tell him if he asked, only he never does.

This time she's still in bed, raised up and listening, her whole body taut.

'What's up?'

Since yesterday it has become impossible for him to call her darling, and everything else has suddenly become impossible as well.

Marguerite whispers: 'He's in the bathroom again.'

Who is? Castleton asks her crossly: 'What're you on about?'

She signals furiously to him not to make a noise. 'Pass me my chemise!'

She snatches it from him. Her look dares him to follow her out of bed. 'Stay where you are and get my brother.' She orders harshly : 'Put out that light!'

All *right*. Keep your shirt on! He's groping blindly for the phone. Before he has made his connection he hears the door of Marguerite's bathroom open and shut.

Hullo. He has caught a familiar whiff of cologne. His brother-in-law is standing beside him in the dark.

'I was just trying to get you. What the hell's going on?'

'It's puss. Let's go,' says Benoir.

Somebody must have alerted him. He has been put in the picture. He is also fully dressed. It is this second fact which to Castleton is somehow the more alarming.

They go through the dark room without a word to stand like conspirators outside the bathroom door. No light is showing under it. There's no light showing any-where.

Benoir knocks softly, once. 'Mi?'

There is no answer, though they can hear her in there moving about.

Silly bitch! Castleton pushes open the door. At once a bullying voice warns them : 'No light!'

They can just make her out crouching in front of something rolled-up in a corner.

'Shut the door!' They might be looking for a gas leak. Castleton switches on the light and immediately George shoots out of his hiding place and into a new position.

'Fools! Idiots! Bastards! I said, No light!' She rounds on them like a horse coper, abusing them both in her rage at her dying son.

'Come out, d'you hear? Come out, or I will beat you like a carpet!'

He doesn't turn a hair. He seems quite friendly squatting there eyeing them all from his splendid new position. He even yawns from time to time.

'Wait till I get you out,' his mother promises. 'You'll be surprised at what you'll get!'

'Don't tell me,' George answers saucily. 'You know I adore surprises.'

'You slut! Come out before I drag you out by your hair!'

'Somebody shut her up,' Castleton says.

'Yes, shut up, Mi.' Her brother tells her shortly: 'You are getting on everyone's nerves with that noise. We are trying to get puss out for you. Now leave us in peace.' He's down on his knees trying to coax George out. By lying full length on the floor he has just managed to reach an ankle. 'Come on out, baby.'

'Non, je ne veux pas,' George says, yawning. He has squeezed himself into a tiny space between the wash-stand and the wall. He looks very pretty, yawning and blinking his eyes at them all.

' 'Allo,' remarks George as if he hadn't spotted Castleton before.

'Hullo to you. What about coming out?'

'No, I don't want to,' answers George, experimentally closing one eye.

'Mais si, mais si,' insists his uncle. 'You want to come to maman.'

Castleton cheerily backs him up: 'Course you do, ducky.'

'No,' answers George with finality. He leaves the eye shut.

'Aren't you ashamed to make your poor mother so unhappy?' Benoir wants to know.

He stops yawning to look at her with interest. 'What will she do if I come out?'

Nothing. They will carry him back to his room so that he can rest. In his nice bed.

That is the trouble. He doesn't want to rest in his nice bed any more. He bargains warily: 'In Mimi's bed?'

Certainly in Mimi's bed.

'What about him? Will he be in it?' George indicates Castleton.

By all means. If George likes.

O, yes, he does like. Very much. 'Who else is coming?'

Whoever he chooses. It's up to him.

He chooses his uncle and his Tante Marie and Mado and Ouisti and little Miss. That's not counting his mother and her husband. 'I have forgotten his name but, anyway, I think you know him. He's British or something,' says George.

Mr Castleton.

'Something like that,' says George.

His uncle assures him that Mr Castleton is a very good friend of the family, and that everyone so far listed will be with him in bed with the possible exception of Tante Marie who is souffrante and is on that account obliged to retire rather early.

'O, yes, I know,' George nods his head. He is being reasonable about it. He has even started to uncoil himself a little.

'Will Viv be here?'

'Of course.'

'When?'

Quite soon. His cousin is probably on the road at this moment.

Probably? 'Ah, si c'est comme ça, vous savez.' He is obviously having second thoughts.

'Will you let us take you back to bed now?'

No. If that is all they have to offer he would rather stay where he is.

'Oh *God*!' calls out Marguerite.

'I'll get him for you,' Castleton says. He still hates her, but he hates still more to see her cry like that.

'Come on, old love,' says Castleton.

George tells him crossly: 'Non, je vous ai déjà dit.'
He is busy completing arrangements for retracting into his hole.

'Pull him out!' Marguerite calls. 'Pull him out by his legs!'

They are all on the floor now, grovelling in their efforts to winkle him out of his hole. Castleton notes with satisfaction even Mim's doing it.

Only George is finding it funny to kick their hands away.

'You idiot!' It has suddenly got too much for Marguerite and she is blaming Castleton for everything. 'Why do you meddle with things that don't concern you? If you can't do the job properly, get out and let my brother do it!'

Terrific. And after that he's bloody welcome to it. *And* the rest.

But Benoir has another problem. He has just discovered a bloodstain on his cuff. He tells his sister shortly: 'Less noise. And get up from the floor. That is the first thing,' Benoir tells her. Merde. Where has it come from? Up till now he had been quite certain there had been no sign of blood. Actually, now he's looking for it, there's quite a lot of it around. Most of it's on the floor by the washstand.

So that is where he got it from. Merde. He asks, as a matter of interest: 'Are they standing by in there?'

He means the medical team. 'They're supposed to be standing by.'

They're in the bedroom. 'I'll get them,' Castleton says. He has spotted the bloodstains and so has Marguerite.

For several seconds she seems unable to take it in.

'Keep quiet, please,' her brother warns her. But she starts screaming: 'There is blood! There is blood on the floor!'

He agrees with her fully. Naturally there is blood. Puss has obviously had a nose bleed. 'Stop it, Mi,' says her brother. She is so wrapped round his neck he can neither see nor hear.

He points out: 'You are damaging your chances, my dear.' She is not capable of reason.

He says: 'You must let go of me, Marguerite. I will try to get your son out for you, but first you must let go.' Benoir assures her: 'I shall do nothing with you draped round my neck.' He asks her, smiling: 'C'est fini, Mi?'

She lets him go. Those two are total anathema, Castleton decides. The kid is awful, too. They're all in it together, and the sooner it's over the better as far as Castleton's concerned, and at the moment he means all of it.

Let them get on with it. He's not interested any more.

But the united French are terrific and are getting him out of his hole with the minimum fuss. He comes scrambling out, looking more debauched than ever because of a bloody nose but very pleased to see them all the same. 'Ham I going to 'ave a bath?' He is a bit confused as to who they all are and what are their intentions, but seems perfectly happy to go along with Marguerite.

'What is she crying for?' he asks them curiously. There is a bubble of blood fluttering in his left nostril that fills and flattens as he breathes. No one has dared to lift him and Marguerite is guiding him step by step towards her bed. He gets as far as the door and stops.

'O, look,' exclaims George in a surprised voice. The bubble has distended to a balloon which grows bigger and bigger and bursts. There is a hard pattering sound as another balloon pops out and bursts on to the marble floor like someone spitting out of a window. And suddenly there's a whole mob of them taking aim, spitting and spattering, plipping and plopping on to the heated marble.

In seconds they are all skating on it, a huge rink of mucus and blood that is spreading over the entire floor as they chase after the wildly panicking child. He evades them, shrieking: 'No! No! I don't want you!' and trying to reach his mother.

A doctor with another behind him skates in and joins the scrum. Two nurses follow them up.

Now all the skaters are bumping into each other, vociferating, yelling instructions, changing direction and charging about like a posse of Keystone cops trying to force an arrest.

'Maman! Maman!'

'Moumou!'

They fall into each other's arms. He is still pumping it out, covering himself and Marguerite. They look as if they'd murdered each other and are standing aghast at the other's deed.

Now the cops have all converged and are holding each other in a fast-breathing clinch, while at the core the human gusher is being forcibly turned off.

He exists for a while longer, taking his time and slaying them all while he turns from an aggressive pink to the defeated blue of cyanosis. Even now it's not over. He has suffered so much he is neither male nor female or old or young or anything except still not dead.

The crowd has tramped off to the bedroom leaving the bathroom brightly lit and silent.

An enormous black fly, like a flying moustache, zooms in through a window hitting itself against ceiling and walls in its excitement to get at some trodden-in towels. It climbs up the heap and down again, black as a hat, marching and feeding till it suddenly drops like a stone into the slurry of parboiled blood on the newly vacated floor of the rink.

Marguerite and her half-dead boy are inextricably fused, a small double-headed Medusa, hair snaked with sweat, rolled up in the middle of the bed.

A desolate sound issues from one of the mouths like a weak mewling.

'Oh, darling,' Castleton calls out. 'Oh, darling darling girl.' But as he comes near, one of the heads whips round and shoots a lethal ray in his direction from blazing hallowe'en eyes. The other head remains impassively turned away, eyes closed, indifferent to them all except Marguerite.

He hears his brother-in-law saying, 'It's finished. You can look.'

Only a vestige of the struggle remains. The mere sigh of a cry that faints as it flies and is lost in a hole in the air. He has turned into a separate being again, the leached head happy and comforted on Marguerite's breast. The pretty snowy features are composed in a small, clever smile. He has accepted everything.

Castleton looks and looks.

The knowing fly from the bathroom shoots in for a minute in a high state of excitement looking for more towels.

It has actually brought another one with it. They case the joint quickly in their moustachy way, then dart off to the equatorial bathroom where towels beyond their wildest dreams are waiting for them, and time still stands at their lucky hour of two a.m. on the 5th of August in Paris.

20

Hurrying to the Field of Paris

The Bienvilles are hurrying to the field of Paris in his beautiful fast Lamborghini. He wants to try her out, so he's kidded himself it's quicker than flying.

His wife is with him. He *wants* her with him. She's in his scheme of things. She's on his side. It's going to be all right. It's so good to be going home he could die.

He likes his wife. He was planning on driving all the way to the Ritz with his hand on her fanny but the beautiful fast Lamborghini won't let him. That sexy control panel always gets between. It's an hélas, because he likes his wife's fanny which he has recently christened Enid after an early English governess of Thingo's, much prized by Bienville for her British teeth.

Oh, yes, he likes his wife. He likes her (dyed) grey eyes, he likes her pointy-pink elbows like the snouts of blind, white mice. He still doesn't like her minimouse nails. But he's going to be a good boy and speak French to his wife because his wife can fluently not speak any number of languages including French.

Also he will be a good boy and not spoil her act,

because by now she will have convinced herself that she is being a power house of strength to her hubby in his hour of trial and so her morale is very high.

Also by now she's probably thinking about that good gravy hubby will inherit. She's hung around the de Grenier woods too long not to be thinking about gravy for most of her waking life. It has been Thought for the Day with her family ever since it was leaked that a certain event was imminent. So stick around for the laughs when Thingo doesn't die.

It's going to be all right. He knows it. He has the radio full on because of it. He jokes the whole way with his wife. They exchange lighted cigarettes. He loves her. She loves him. They love each other.

'Your father will be pleased to see you.'

Bienville predicts: 'He'll throw me out on my ass. They keep a pack of brutes especially for it at the Ritz.'

'Brutes?'

'Dogs. Bow-wow,' barks Bienville in French.

'Oh, you are funny,' squeals Elaine. She's mad about belonging to this curious person of whom she knows practically nothing and about whose family she knows even less. She only knows they are astronomically rich, she has no real idea of where they come from. Fred told her his people came originally from Central France. Dijon or Clermont-Ferrand, she has forgotten which, but she knows they owned silk mills and were already wealthy by the time they fled to Martinique from Paris at the time of the Revolution.

There was another revolution in Martinique so the Benoirs had had to fly again, this time to Louisiana which, at that time, Fred says, was a French colony like the Place Vendôme before they sold it to the British. He says the Benoirs all got those peculiar complexions from living in the tropics. Also it seems they are partly Chinese with a lot of German blood which is why, Fred says, they call themselves the Sioux. But when Elaine told Fred she couldn't see the connection he had agreed with her at once.

Elaine loves Fred. She loves his impudent features. Lips, eyelids, neat close ears, everything the same outlandish colour, a sort of tan, as if they had been dyed. Une vraie gueule à claquer with its tomcat smile, and those long eyes that never express anything she can understand.

He is shorter than she is, and two years younger, but even this she finds charming. Her *cadet-mari* with his lively hands and the cocky stance of his feet which are smaller than hers. His voice, too, excites her. It's harsh like the voice of an exotic bird, and his violet-black hair reminds her of plumage.

This is the celebrated 'blue' hair of the Benoirs who are, Fred swears, direct descendants of Gilles de Rais. He has never explained the connection and she has never asked for fear of inciting his scorn. If there is one thing Fred despises it's a fool. Fred despises nearly everything, Elaine has discovered, and absolutely everyone who is not a Sioux.

He's really snob about this, and if she ever tries to tell him anything about her family he simply turns the radio up till she stops.

He's terribly clever, and a total enigma, and she loves driving through the night with him, feeding him endless

cigarettes while his right hand explores her left breast
and his eyes unswervingly read the road.

'What are you thinking about?'

'Marie.'

He knows it half kills her to hear him say that name
which isn't actually cerebral, even for her, but great for
him because like that he can bug her blind about that
alleged relationship she has been trying to sniff out and
put on the spot ever since this marriage he has got himself into, don't ask him why.

She's too average to start anything new. She just keeps
warming over everything she has ever heard. Picking over
faded old forget-me-nots like: 'Why d'you always call
your cousin by that name if his real name is Georges?
Has he always been sick? Of course I'm sorry, Fred,
but what a pity he can't go to boarding school. It must be
difficult for his mother not to spoil him. Why d'you
like him so much? I find him extraordinary, not like a
child at all. Why did you take your hand away, Fred?'
asks Elaine.

He's waiting till she quits on shlocking the pimade.

'Pimade?' echoes his wife who, Bienville likes to think,
knows less about anything than anyone else on earth.

Pimade. Pimento sauce. The gunk they rubbed into a
nigger's ass after a flogging. It was designed to hurt, says
Bienville, so she can quit on the chicane with his
cousin.

He shouts at her: 'Don't try to be intellectual with me,
de Grenier. Just tell it as it is, you're jealous.'

Jealous? How can she be jealous of a boy? She's hoping to glean something from what he'll say to that, but
he just answers calmly: 'Marie's a lot.'

Elaine thinks sulkily, even a little's too much of that kid. He reminds her of those awful wax flowers in provincial cemeteries. So unhealthy and spoiled to death. She'll never forget that drive down to Biarritz when he came with them. Fred had let the chauffeur drive while they sat in the back with his cousin. Those two had giggled the whole way down without addressing a single word to her. They had a kind of private language. And at the restaurant where they stopped for lunch she noticed the whole time they were touching each other under the table.

Her entire stay at Biarritz had been ruined.

Her in-laws! What an extraordinary bunch! Her father-in-law does his best to be pleasant, but she thinks it would be impossible for anyone to really get to know him. He is supposed to have a different mistress for every day. And not all are from good families. Fred told her in confidence once his father has une nostalgie de la boue. No wonder Fred's mother is peculiar. Completely helpless and half deaf on top of it. Fred says his father chooses all her clothes for her and that she is terrified of meeting people. There is another brother, Baudoin, a cripple whom so far she has only seen once, at her wedding. But worst of all is that aunt of Fred's, Marguerite Castleton, the mother of Georges Benoir. She has only quite recently married again – for the third time! At least her husband is English and polite, but she is the rudest and most arrogant person Elaine has ever met. She is also unbelievably chic. Elaine is thankful that she and Fred are going to live on the other side of Paris. She wouldn't last five minutes in that ménage. She steals a look at her husband. She hopes he hasn't guessed what she's been thinking of. She forces herself to say : 'I hope you'll find your cousin better, Fred.'

He answers promptly : 'He's probably dead.'

He has almost certainly guessed, and now he's going to punish her for it. Already he has slewed his eyes round to her hair.

She calls out defensively : 'It's exactly the same style as Marguerite's. I even went to her man. I thought it would please you. Since you admire your aunt so much.'

'On you,' says Bienville, 'it looks strictly non-colossal. I think you should know it,' Bienville says earnestly and turns his full attention to the road.

She starts to cry but he's not worried. You can always dry de Grenier tears on a good thick wad of folding money.

Meanwhile they are nearing the field of Paris and when they get there he is going to ask Nap outright and once for all how it is with his cousin Marie, that love trick he has to get back in his life again. And if he does this Marie won't die. He will not turn all those funky colours with that kind of a slatey radiance like a black rainbow, but stick around with his Mr Viv and that will be the big purple time for them both.

Shucking out sugar-beans for ever and ever.

'Marie, vous êtes comme une vase de cristal le plus pur.'

'What did you say ?'

'I said get out. We're here.' She must have caught his lips moving. He guides his car into the drive but finds it difficult to park, there are so many others there. The courtyard is stuffed with them, while a scarlet vapour rises from hundreds of salvias under their concentrated lights.

Medics, thinks Bienville, getting out. He slams the door. Sweet Jesus Christ. The Ritz is blazing like a factory.

'What is the matter, Fred?'

He signals her to get back into the car.

'Has something happened?'

'Goof off,' says Bienville. The sweat is standing on his forehead. He tries the lodges first. He can see lights blazing behind plate-glass and ironwork grills, but no dogs bark and all remains shut and unresponsive to his passionate ringing.

Looks like the bag-out has commenced. We have a horizontal here, thinks Bienville. I can smell it.

He goes round to the main entrance, and keeps his finger on the bell. At once his mother's little dog starts yapping. A shadow from somewhere inside the hall comes swimming quickly towards him. The heavy plate-glass door swings open and Benoir himself is standing there. He isn't carrying Ouistiti. Not good. When Benoir quits on toting Ouisti it's bad.

'Hiya, Herman, since when you been put on the doors?' asks Bienville, who doesn't want to know. There is a point beyond which a thing's not funny and they are clearly at it.

A voice he barely recognizes as his father's says: 'Shut the door.'

He shuts it, expostulating: 'What's with Marie, Papa? Is he worse or better or what? I tried to phone you since a whole week. I never got put through. I mean to *any-one*,' Bienville says. 'What's this new set-up at the Ritz, anyways? What happened with the conciergerie tonight?

I rang and rang. Positively nothing.' Bienville declares : 'I just don't get the scene.'

'Don't talk any more,' advises his father.

Sez which? 'I have a lot of dialogue for you.' He takes a step in Benoir's direction and gets a smack across his face which sends him into the wall. He comes up gasping. 'Well, *thanks*! Wonderful to know you really *care*!' He manages to retrieve his smile, but Nap's clever little mitt shoots out and knocks it off again with a most educated slap.

Wham! That was for real, all right! 'Hey, Hermie, that was *me*!'

'Shut up,' says Benoir, and comes for him again.

'You outa your skull?' Bienville would like to know. He has bitten his tongue and he is shaking with fury. 'I ask you about Marie and you start kicking the jam.'

'Good night,' says Benoir. He has opened the door for Bienville. You have only to look at him now to get the scene in one. Bienville bursts into terrible sobs.

His father informs him calmly : 'Your cousin died at two o'clock this morning. He cried for you yesterday afternoon and we told him you were coming. But in the end he only wanted his mother. So it's really not important that you weren't here. Stop crying, Viv,' counsels Benoir and walks away.

The hall is very quiet. Only the open door remains waiting for Bienville. He rushes through it, leaving it open behind him.

In the courtyard the cars are still waiting and the Ritz is still blazing into the growing daylight. He hurls his bloodied handkerchief into the salvias. He wants to vomit.

He wants to bomb the Ritz. He'd like to overturn and set fire to every last damn car, including his own.

His wife is asleep in the passenger seat in a private slum of tissues, toilet preparations, cigarettes and lighters. The heater is full on.

She wakes up as he plunges in beside her, rocking the whole machine and sweeping her debris on to the floor. She asks him sleepily: 'What's the time? How is your cousin? What's the news?'

The news is supercolossal. He slams the heater off and backs out of the courtyard, purposely bumping as many cars as he can.

He shoots off south again, tearing up the kilometres in his rage to put as many as fast as he can between himself and the Ritz.

Elaine asks uneasily: 'What is the matter with your face?' She has become alarmed by his cryptic mud-coloured mask and the blank stones of his eyes. 'Has something happened, Fred?'

Half a mile down the road he answers her. 'My cousin died. Other than that it's okay.' Bienville says: 'So do me a solid and wrap it.'

'I'm so sorry, Fred.'

'You move me.' He switches the radio on to get the first programme of the day.

'Look out for some place we can have breakfast. Keep looking,' Bienville tells her. If she looks at him now he'll destroy her.

21

Par Avion

It appears this is the two-hundred-and-forty-sixth letter received by her in the week immediately following the death. She hasn't kept count, they have done it for her, but it seems that all these outpourings have actually been filed pending the attention of that madman her brother, who, with the help of his secretaries, intends to answer them all!

'By the time you've signed your full name two hundred times or whatever it is, you'll have your right arm in plaster, mon vieux!'

She suggests a pen-name for him: 'Gaga'. It's short and in her opinion exactly illustrates his present frame of mind. He merely asks if she would like him to read a certain letter to her.

'Why, is it different from any of the others?' These letters have come from all over the world, some of them from total strangers. Other bereaved mothers, for example. Sisters in sorrow. She needn't tell him she can't wait not to read those.

'I am not asking you to.'

Or letters from fanatics who have prayed for moumou day and night and now insist on transferring their attentions to her. 'Thank you for nothing,' says Marguerite. He points out: 'This is from Vince's brother.'

'That's bad,' says Marguerite.

He starts to read in what she always thinks of as Benoir's 'holy' voice. All emotion down to a minimum for fear of reopening her wound!

The notion that she could be upset by the vicarious sufferings of virtual strangers is making her want to laugh. Really, poor fellow, he is even refraining from smoking!

'Our treasured Mim. . . .'

She is giggling already, but he goes on: 'It's quite beyond me to express what my darling girl and I felt when we got Vin's sad cable. . . .'

'Did I open my mouth?' Marguerite protests.

'. . . but though we know we can never hope to make up for the loss of your darling little chap, yet it may bring you a tiny grain of comfort to know that though we only saw him once we all of us most dearly loved him.'

'That poor moumou,' sighs Marguerite, 'so many people to love him!'

'. . . Our darling Vin told us when we spoke to him last week that you are being miraculously brave. He thinks that when you are more rested and can make the effort you will probably want a complete change of scene, but, precious girl, *do* tell him that my Syb and I would adore nothing better than for you both to come and stay with us, either in town or at Ashwater, whichever you choose. For as long as you like. For good if you could bear us. As long as we're together, darling, that's what counts. Dear old Vin seems quite stunned by this shocking blow that has fallen on us all, but darling heart, we know he'll be a tower of strength to you as will your own two dear brothers.

'. . . Everyone adores you, Mim darling, never lose sight of that.

'Our fond love to you as always, Sybil and Cecil.'

She doesn't stir.

'Eh, bien, Mi.'

She asks in a surprised voice : *'Tiens*, it's not finished ?'

Yes, it is finished. He asks her coldly : 'Are you going to answer it ?'

'What for ?' asks Marguerite.

This letter is from Vince's brother.

'And Syb,' Marguerite reminds him stoutly.

'Whatever you think of it, I think you should answer it, Mi.'

She doesn't remotely dream of it. 'You answer it. With all the others. You are my tower of strength,' says Marguerite. 'It says so in the letter.'

'Mi, are you going to be serious or not ?'

Not. 'Leave me alone with your damn Castletons. They can feel as much as they like about my son as long as I don't have to hear about it. I can stand everything but their sympathy. Their English soothing syrup.'

She calls out vehemently : 'No more regrets. J'en ai tellement assez tu m'entends ? Je m'en fous de ces gens. Let them leave my son in peace.'

He takes back the letter and says formally : 'In that case I shall answer it for you.'

'Do what you like, but leave me alone.'

He will write at once, and afterwards when she is calmer they can discuss her future intentions.

'Intentions?'

Towards her husband. He sees no possible advantage in her continuing the relationship as it exists. She shrugs. He advises her: 'Stop it, Mi. And try to patch it up. He's terribly unhappy.'

As long as he doesn't unload it on her. That's all she asks. She remembers suddenly. He hadn't one scrap of flesh on his bones. Not one. None. When he was bleeding to death she had called out to him: Tu es mon beau lys blanc. Tu es mon premier et mon dernier désir – and it hadn't made a difference by a single drop of his blood.

'No, it's not possible,' says Marguerite, 'it simply isn't possible to accept one single word more of sympathy.'

22

A Negotiated Peace

Benoir has come up with what is probably the only naïve suggestion he has made in his life. The suggestion is that he and Mim and Benoir, presumably acting as ref, should all betake themselves to a neutral spot, with a view to determining a possible future for the Castletons' foundering marriage.

The spot with the view is Switzerland. Just who this scheme is for only Benoir can tell. The marriage has been dead for yonks and everyone knows it.

Still an' all, it shows that warmth still lingers amongst the ashes of their own personal relationship, so Castleton has agreed to go along with Benoir's two-day Summit. What Mim's reaction was he has no means of knowing. They've hardly been talking since the Rink. She probably swore at him like a market-porter for his pains, but she'll still be along. She loves her brother more than anyone else in the world, nearly as much as she had loved her son. Perhaps as much, and he wouldn't be surprised, as she had loved her first and, for any practical purpose, only husband.

What a funny lady.

Meanwhile Benoir has been working like a gallant little beaver to get his peace negotiations off the ground and at the same time, to coin a phrase, to leave the Ritz as he would wish to find it. Marie is his chief concern, of course. Her well-being has always been of paramount importance to Benoir, and it's a gauge of his affections for the Castletons that he should leave her, even for two days, in an attempt to salvage their beastly marriage.

All good stuff, thinks Castleton ungratefully, as on the eve of the Summit, at about six o'clock, he makes tracks for Benoir's office. He wants a picture of George to take away with him. The Summit's a non-starter as far as he's concerned, and he has no intention of ever coming back to Paris, so a photo of Mim's chap is what he's after. His most Catholic Majesty, Georges-Marie Armand Benoir.

It's funny how he has given up thinking of George in even the remotest relationship to himself. It hadn't always been so. Time was in Vol. I, he horridly recalls, when he had really carried on about Mim's chap, busily appointing himself Mentor, Philosopher and Friend, till even the kindly Dauphin had plainly thought he was barmy.

Now all he wants is a photograph of George. He hangs about, getting in everyone's way while they try to dig something out of the files for him.

Benoir unearths the very thing : 'portrait of puss before you knew him. Take it, fella.'

Puss before Castleton knew him was full of spunk. At five years old, in the now famous white sailor suit his sex appeal was zooming and not a whisker of his disaster was anywhere to be seen.

'No thanks, no rubbish,' Castleton says rudely.

He looks at other pictures, taking his time. He must be looking at every photograph taken of the Dauphin since birth. The choice is enormous, giving unlimited scope for venting his spleen against the Sioux. He is gabby and argumentative about everything, and wilfully mistakes a picture of Benoir, aged eight, for the pleasure of hearing him say, 'I'm afraid that isn't puss, fella.'

'Go *on*, don't give me *that*,' says Castleton knowingly. He's delighted to see how thoroughly he already is on everybody's nerves and hangs on to the picture for ages while the search goes on for something to make him let go. He loafs about, taking stock of everything, studying a jokey picture of Armand and Mim as delectable adolescents dressed up in each other's clothes for a fashionable charity ball.

'Good lor'.'

'D'you want it?'

No fear. 'What about cuttings?' asks Castleton, pretending sudden inspiration.

Cuttings?

Newspaper clippings. Of George. Some of these press photos are jolly good. 'Ever so lifelike,' Castleton says.

The trouble with press clippings is that they don't last. . . .

'Who wants them to?' asks Castleton nastily.

. . . they fade, disintegrate. Escape, as one could almost call it, into the original pulp.

'That is the worst aspect,' points out his brother-in-law.

Unless it's the best. 'I'll settle for this one,' Castleton says. He has picked a real lulu from *Paris Match*.

It was taken on the steps of the St Esprit, immediately

after the Dauphin's first, and also last, communion. Hands, coming from all directions, support him from every side. It's quite obvious he can no longer stand.

'His Most Catholic Majesty,' says Castleton. He's pleased at the flush he has brought to his brother-in-law's face.

Benoir says simply : 'Choose another one.' He is showing the whites of his eyes.

'No, I like this one.' Castleton thinks perversely : Hooray. I'm on his wick at last. They get it out of the file for him in silence and put it in an envelope. He amuses himself, meanwhile, by reading out old society news. All the snob events of Vol. I, like his and Mim's wedding, and the wedding of young Benoir. Soc cock, but he has read a lot of it aloud before he packs it in.

The secs have done their prep and dug a massive amount of data out. But there's recent stuff here, too, my goodness yes, it's *all* there isn't it, with 'Hope for the Dauphin' and 'Mr Wonderful brings new faith to stricken relatives.'

He tries to picture the Sioux as stricken but can't. He's ever so stricken if it interests anyone, but it doesn't.

On to the funny stuff : 'Georges-Marie Benoir,' reads Castleton. 'Slight response to treatment. Renal complications give rise to anxiety.'

From the renal to the regal : 'The magnificent Paris apartment of Mrs H. Vincent Castleton is to be sold by private treaty at the end of the month. The sale is to include the striking murals executed by the Spanish artist, Sandor. They are expected to realize in the neighbourhood of a quarter of a million pounds.'

Fascinating stuff.

'The flat, which has never been occupied since its completion, was to have been the Paris home of Mr and Mrs Castleton.

'A spokesman said today the chief presumed reason for the sale is the sudden death of Georges-Marie Benoir, only child of Mrs Castleton by her previous marriage at sixteen to her sportsman-millionaire cousin, Georges Benoir. The boy would have been ten in a few days' time.'

Ten.

He takes the photo handed to him without a word of thanks and walks to the door. Ten. The spokesman said so.

Benoir calls after him: 'If you have nothing of importance on we could take a stroll in the garden before dinner.'

'No, thanks, ducky,' Castleton calls back.

'It's a splendid evening.'

'Rats. Don't ruddy patronize me. Shut up, Benoir.'

Ten. He would have been ten in a few days' time. A spokesman had said so. But Benoir had ruled out even one day more by saying an operation would depend on a quite different set of circumstances to those which, in fact, had existed at the time.

He hates Benoir even worse than he hates the spokesman.

23

The Solid Plan

They have moved into their new apartment and Elaine is carrying his child. She has just told him so. He finds both facts equally depressing.

'Where are you going, Fred?' shrieks out the nut he's married to, still loyal to the belief that it is English and smart to call everyone Fred.

'You're not reaching me, baby,' Bienville says, and strides across the room.

He hears his wife call after him prophetic tidings like: 'You will catch a chill!'

He is glad quickly to shut himself out on the terrace and turn the key. He knows exactly what he is going to do but stands for a moment staring at the moon which is swimming quickly in and out and round about the cloudscapes and out into deep channels of the open sky again.

The nut is knocking frantically on glass but he remains motionless in his blue corner, teeth and eyes lit white by the racing moon, cigarette sparking furiously in the exact centre of his neat, wicked smile.

He is seriously reviewing the recent behaviour, towards himself, of his father. About your personality problem, Benoir, thinks Bienville, genuinely shocked by his findings.

Benoir has acted like a crud. Not only on that special night Bienville still can't get himself to think about, but at the funeral. Plus three weeks later he's still handing out the horse manure with his frozen silences, his directifs, his mandats royaux.

Do this. Do that. Move it, hear me? Get the lead outa your ass.

Pas sympa. Pas du tout chic. For this there will be a slight service charge is Bienville's verdict.

So while a blue-faced moon is fossicking head first in a torn pillow of a cloud, Bienville brings out the gun.

The cloud is also blue, so the darkness is temporarily on, which is okay with Bienville who has this solid plan : when the moon shoots suddenly backwards out of that cloud he will put it in his mouth and do it.

Meanwhile the dark is on, so Bienville is more or less thinking about his wife who is so average it could be minutes before she connects after the shot and comes running out exclaiming : 'I love him, I love him,' and 'How did it happen?' in her cute slumberwear to find her only husband dead and looking it.

The darkness is lifting. Already he can see the glare as the moon's rim comes scrambling out of the frayed cloud.

Now. Killed as in dead. But the moon is on the run again and he still hasn't done it.

He'd be cool to call it off. The chump thing is to do it. There must be some way to reverse but he can't find one.

As from today it has suddenly all been strung out on
Benoir. That turned on, lip giving, pretty little bougre is
sure due for one awful switching.

So, whatever it's like when it happens, it can't be all
bad, because Bienville can run most of it off against
Nap, against Tante and the whole of the Sioux (Paris)
Ltd.

But especially will he add it to his score against his
cousin, the late li'l Marie. The late, late li'l Marie.

He is surprised to find he has a hard-on. He has only
to say aloud: 'That li'l Marie was for me' and immediately the assault course is on. He says it again.

Hey: it's funnier than funny him talking to his dick
like this. It's extra because this is where the grin could
really start. If his stand holds till his wife finds him there
will be absolutely no prizes for guessing who he was
thinking of at the end.

When he was not. Because the one subject he will be
studying to the very end is the gall of that clapped out
Benoir and that last special hand-out Bienville is crazy
for still.

'So I will get him out of my hair,' announces Bienville,
'on account I do not go for dandruff too much.' The dick
is getting really interested at things. It is really involved.
The air blows disagreeably on his heated flesh. He rises
cautiously in case it takes a dive, but it stays with him as
he moves, step by step, from the dark overhang of the
balcony above and out into the open by the glittering
balustrade where the moon is now pouring vaporous light
into a sky-blue sky with such abrasive intensity that all
its rays are broken off short.

His aim now is to pop in sync. Top tip if you have

ever to shoot yourself for being nominated Garbage of the Year by your hilarious but still authentic father.

Associated cold front moving in now. Overall low due early p.m. tomorrow when Hermie, in his English motor, crosses the Swiss border and gets the French headlines full in the teeth.

'Le jeune Benoir se suicide pendant la nuit Samedi ou Dimanche.'

'La mort de "Viv" Benoir était confirmée à Paris hier soir.' But 'Benoir: Le jour tragique d'un père' from the *Cri du Peuple* is the one that's going to slay him. It's so corny it's ridiculous, but that has never yet stopped pop publicity from killing Benoir dead.

'I have a père tragique,' Bienville explains. 'Some people's pères have professions and things, but mine is simply tragique.'

Boy, it's crazy the way that thing responds to his voice. It is practically turning red, white and blue at the sound.

'My father is Arsy Herman,' Bienville says. 'He is a fully lapsed member of the Catholic faith. I do not like him on account he is extremely sincere. He is also a rake and a necrophile as well as a pocket Adonis of exceptionally 1er Choix.

'I despise necrophiles. Particularly any necrophiles who are also pocket Adonises I totally despise. I do not accept they are tragique. My tool is also deeply unconvinced. I have a very educated tool,' says Bienville, 'a kind of a chic-dick-smart-banana who declines this whole theory of the père tragique.'

So if Benoir wants to prove something he should start

right in to be tragique now, because as far as Bienville is concerned it is very much hier soir already.

'That Benoir bores me,' Bienville says. 'I mean, he really *bores* me. You'd think he'd be thankful Thingo's dead and has finally quit bugging him, so he can for pete's sake stop identifying him with his mother every single breath that Thingo ever drew. But when he died she died again. So she died twice for Benoir. And here he is such a dedicated little necrophile, and suddenly there are two stiffs for him to love.'

Bienville calls out: 'I know your sort, mista, and you bore me dead' – and pow! So while the dick is doing everything for him but read and write, Bienville puts into action his plan for bringing off both weapons at once.

It makes a noise, but that is more because he brings a table down with him.

'Papa,' says Bienville, who had meant to call out meaningful things as he fell like 'Remember the Alamo!' After that, nothing. Only the quiet of the balcony with the pale blue tables and chairs, and the glittering balustrade and floor and everything made of powdered diamonds under the motionless downpour of steely rain from a moon very high up in the fathomless sky.

24

Notice to Persons Arriving from Abroad

As they near the French border it begins to rain, as usual. My God, she'll be glad to leave France where the weather has become as demoralized as everything else.

One thing she has promised herself, she is going to leave Paris without a word to her friends. Since they all seem to think they had a legitimate claim to her son, it will at least make one less excursion to the wailing wall for her if she goes without saying good-bye.

Benoir will, of course, despise her for it, but that is one thing she won't let him force her into, even if it gets her a worse press than usual. As to that, another zero won't finish her off. Ever since moumou's death Benoir has held an almost permanently bad opinion of her.

Oh, she can't wait till this whole mess of the divorce and Vincent's brat is cleared up and done with, and she can begin to live again in Buenos Aires. She's still sulking about Benoir's refusal to make an Italian detour, and is cheering herself up by dwelling on a certain incident she will never be able to tell anyone about except perhaps

Beau, much later on. Certainly not now, and certainly not Benoir. She is really afraid when she thinks what he might do if it ever got to his ears she had seen what had happened between him and his son on the night of the death when Bienville had come too late to see his cousin, and Benoir had taught him a lesson at last.

She smiles under cover of keeping her head turned to the road.

Piff! Paff! That last one had been a beauty. A really juicy one right across the mouth. She had watched it all from the head of the stairs.

And not before time. There should have been more to follow. Her blood still boils when she thinks of the tricks that delinquent has been up to since a child. . . . He had been as mischievous as a monkey, but Benoir had never lifted a finger to discipline him.

Well, now he has seen the result of his 'liberal' education. It's too late, but at least he has seen the need for a radical change in policy.

In her opinion it's not the only policy he needs to change. If he doesn't come to his senses soon he will be served the same with his clinics.

Whatever he thinks, they have already started to drink his blood. With their exigencies, their never-ending demands on his intelligence, his nerves, his time. For any other project his money would have been enough, but these damn clinics of his will never be satisfied till they have drained his last drop of blood.

That clinic he is opening in Rabat next year, for instance, she has never heard of anything so sentimental in her life. A dump like that can only be cured in one way. Sterilize, and get rid of the whole population.

In France it's no better, as far as she can see, with half of Paris using the Clinique Benoir as a luxury hotel. After all, why not? No expenses, no responsibilities. They have never had it so good. They would be fools not to avail themselves.

Apart from the fantastic medical side, if one could ignore a money-devouring monster like that, their brats are educated, fed and entertained like princes. Especially now with the new children's wing which, by the way, was completed precisely at the time that moumou's illness had entered its final phase.

Now he has even installed a sterile cinema on top of the TV that is already in every room!

It's not surprising that no one is in a hurry to go home and take up their responsibilities again. With no one to kick them out, they simply park their brats at the Clinique Benoir for as long as they dare.

All this should be a lesson to him, but it is not. Because of Maman's death, Benoir will never be able to dis-associate himself from this filthy disease. Well, she can. She has already done it. It killed their mother and Beau is a cripple for life. Now it has killed her son she's had enough of it. Why should it concern her who else it murders? Let them bury their own dead.

She sneaks a look at his profile. Benoir smiles back.

'What are you growling into your beard about?' enquires her brother.

'Nothing. Why?'

'I know that expression,' says Benoir.

She thinks half proudly: Oh, he loves everyone, that fool! He is exactly like our mother. One has only to go near him to feel it.

Moumou had this same thing in his makeup. Only she had fully made her mind up to knock it out of him before it had time to develop and do him serious harm. One altruist in the family is enough. Not for anything would she have wanted another one like Benoir.

My God, when she thinks of all the filthy tricks she and Beau had played on him when they were all kids together at St Eze. Landing him in hot water with their father had been their favourite sport.

Les deux concierges, Benoir had called them, yet she can't remember a single time when he had seriously lost his temper with them.

It was as if his nine happy years as an adored only child had immunized him for the horrible life he was afterwards condemned to lead at the hands of the terrible conciergerie. Benoir was so much older he always had to be responsible to Papa for whatever went wrong.

It's possible that, with their mother's illness, Papa had too much on his mind. All the same, he could be terribly unfair with Benoir. He should have sent Beau and me packing with a flea in our ear instead of listening to our tales about poor Armand, which in any case were mostly lies.

We seem to have spent our entire lives keeping tabs on his love life! God knows what our governesses were doing!

It's true that Benoir had been extremely precocious, so there was always plenty to report that didn't please Papa.

One thing that surely didn't please him was that her brother's early sexual education was almost entirely in the hands of his own mistresses!

Apparently these ladies had lost no time in reporting

Benoir as an apt and charming pupil who frequently astonished his delighted teachers with his originality and style.

Naturally, the conciergerie had found a nickname for Benoir : 'Le sexuel excédé'. They claimed that whenever he exceeded his own sexual powers he went to confession !

She smiles. Benoir hadn't a vestige of religious feeling left since he was fourteen, but that had never prevented him from pushing his responsibilities on to the Church.

It was a leftover from the time he was never off his knees interceding for Maman and Beau. He was afraid that if he overstepped the mark too often God would let them die to punish him !

This holy period was much admired by the servants. The governesses had held him up as an example to Georges who had literally to be driven to Mass.

Of course, it was all only superstition with Benoir, a kind of bargaining with Heaven.

The moment Maman was dead he completely lost interest. Except for Mass on Christmas Eve, to please Marie, he never goes near a church. Well, he still has his patriotism. That is the one thing salvaged from the general collapse of ideals.

Oh, he is very patriotic is Benoir. It has taken the place of religion with him. He had been quite seriously annoyed with her when she withdrew her custom from the self-styled 'serious' houses of the Rue de la Paix with their boring middle-of-the-road policy, and transferred it to Madrid where they still understand that one doesn't want to look like every rich industrialist's idea of a lady.

'It's up to us to support French industry, Mi,' Benoir had told her gravely.

Her sweet Benoir. She still remembers how furious Papa had been with him because he had insisted on doing his military service. They weren't even living in France at the time. Since Vichy Papa had made no secret of his opinion of the glorious French army!

Oh, his beloved France whose polluted air her brother is already swallowing with such satisfaction.

I will never understand him, thinks Marguerite. She envies him his sunny disposition, his anti-cynicism. Even his absurd patriotism she is jealous of.

She thinks resentfully, Oh, he'll be happy in spite of all of us, that one.

She feels suddenly terribly depressed. She's sorry now that all her life she has contributed, is still contributing, so heavily to his discomfort.

She's afraid of the day when he will say as calmly about her as he had said about Papa after a terrible scene between them. 'Oh, he's impossible, you know, but what d'you expect? No one has told him the truth in all his life, so really it's not surprising.' He had even been amused about it.

A write-off. Marguerite thinks, that's what he thinks about me.

'Armand?'

'What?'

'It is going to be all right in Buenos Aires.'

'There's a lot of optimism about,' her brother observes drily.

'I promise you,' says Marguerite.

He smiles and passes her his cigarette, 'Cheer up, my girl, we are in France.'

He is already thinking about his Paris, his mistress

and his wife. Well, he will never change, so she'll have to be satisfied with whatever stiffening has already been injected into his attitude towards his assassin of a son.

Claque! Good. Very good. And good again. That degenerate had never believed he could really get hurt. That was because he had never once received convincing punishment from anyone. Well, this time his father has convinced him. Marguerite thinks with satisfaction: He's a believer now!

Of course Benoir will forgive him. He has already told her it's valueless to carry punishment beyond a certain point.

For him, perhaps, it's valueless. Never for her. She will hold her spite against Bienville till her last day on earth.

She still wants to laugh out loud every time she thinks how he had rushed out of the house howling, like a spoiled brat who has had his pants taken down for him in no uncertain way.

She thinks quite dispassionately: 'I hope he dies. After his treatment of his cousin I wish him the death of a mad dog.'

Ten minutes later, when they stop at Vallorbe for the French papers, she reads that her wish has come true.

25

Tara the British

So that's the end of the vaunted British-French alliance. Too early yet for either side to examine the components or what, if any, the final damage will be. Fourteen months is all it has taken from the day the boy joined them in New Orleans after the honeymoon up to the day he died on August 5 in Paris.

Paris the 5th of August. The date that nobody from either side will ever forget.

He doesn't want to think about it now. Or about anything else. What he wants now is to sit on in the Bentley and wait for the French to have used their start so that there will be absolutely no chance of his meeting them on the road. Worse still, of seeing the parked Rolls outside a lakeside restaurant and glimpsing the two of them on a private terrace, lunching like lovers. He'll give them an hour. With Benoir's driving they'll be halfway out of Switzerland by then, hellbent for France and their beloved Paris.

They can keep both. Especially they can keep Paris. He never wants to set eyes on the bloody place again.

He wants to get back to London and his own people.
The sooner the better. It's not true, of course, but later
in the day he hopes it will suddenly turn true. Even as
late as London Airport it could happen, or as he was
paying his cab off in front of 38 Wilton Place.

In re No. 38, he'll have to invent a woman for himself
before darling Syb gets busy on his behalf out of the
goodness of her Anglo-Irish heart. He can see himself in
a handsome Knight, Frank and Rutley converted farm-
house with extensive grounds and unbroken views over
the Cotswolds 'getting over' the Sioux with the loving
help of somebody like Sheena Sykes-Bladen, toast of the
Cicester Hunt, bosom pal of darling Syb and now the
second fecund Mrs Castleton.

A rehab in a prefab. Not if I know it, thinks Castleton.

He looks at his watch. Twenty-five minutes to go.
There is no sound except the loud, wet voice of the main
cascade blowing across his solitude from time to time.
He is enjoying his solitude very much. It makes him
feel like the sole survivor of a mine disaster, where, in
some blocked-off gallery after the explosion, the lights
are all still tranquilly burning.

He likes the peaceful post-explosion feeling which is
permitting him to examine in detail this nice Swiss wood.
It's very brown and very green. No birdsong and nothing
much in the way of bloom, either. Only sparse plants of
nettle-leaved bellflowers, so violet in the shade, so wan
in the sun. A rustic seat with built-in litter bin extols
the tidy tourist in proverb and verse. More poker-work
around the bracketed eaves of the Hansel and Gretel
chalet which houses the Damen und Herren, deserted
at this time of day.

A rustic signpost points into the empty dinner-hour wood, promising Schattiger Waldwegs and Café Wirtschafts Biergartens and Herrlicher Ausblicks for the afternoon. The picking and/or uprooting of wild flowers is strictly forbidden. There is a place for everything and everything is in its place except for a solitary chocolate wrapping which is shuffling agitatedly round the rubbish bin, seeking asylum.

A Swiss horse tethered to a log is cropping industriously at the forest floor, mane and tail suddenly transparent in a shaft of sunlight, lips and hips moving rhythmically to its cropping as it moves slowly up the bilberry-carpeted hill, hooves sounding hollow on the hollow-sounding Alp.

Time to go. Punctually at two o'clock the groups of summer visitors from nearby pensions and hotels take up their strolling through the forest rides again. It has suddenly turned very fine and hot and a non-stop flushing and gushing at the Damen und Herren has begun. He's had enough of it. Time to get going.

26

The Gold Tip Pfitzer

An orderly file of transformers marching uphill and down dale, giraffes entering a distant ark, tell him he's on the outskirts of Zurich. Already he has met the traffic, twin torrents of diamonds and rubies flowing side by side in opposite directions, rushing, sliding, standing still.

When he gets to the hotel it's as he thought, the Sioux have already struck camp. The news is broken to him by the manager, M. Anton Fumagali, who also has the honour to report that the more important items of Madame's jewellery have already been expedited to Paris under special security measures.

So that's the official end. All Mim's 'named' pieces. The treasure of the Sioux. All back in Paris where it belongs.

'Any messages?' asks Castleton.

Yes, M. Benoir has left a note. It has already been placed in Mr Castleton's suite.

It'll keep. He knows what's in it, anyway. About a temporary separation being the prudent course, but it need make no difference to their friendship. Luverly stuff.

In Mim's room Pauline, Nicole and a newish woman whose name Castleton has probably never been told are wading through sinking tides of tissue paper packing up Mim's things. Mim's beautiful things. He leaves them to it and steps out into the hotel grounds. Later, when they've finished, he'll get a hotel valet to pack his gear. He doesn't particularly want to be there when the last of Mim's cases are locked.

Beautiful, beautiful Mim.

The hotel grounds are crawling with unpleasant-looking conifers. There's quite a little cemetery of them clambering up the slope. A Breughel-ish troupe of hump-backs and cripples, with tumblers in Arctic blues and silvers, trailing their limbs along the ground. One specially lumpy brute in hodden-green is squatting on the grass, its voluminous valance spread all around is streaked with a custardy yellow simulating gold. An aluminium identity disc says it's a Gold Tip Pfitzer, and serve it right. Crumbs, what a name.

The Sioux don't go in for Gold Tip Pfitzers when burying their dead. They have no use for lugubrious evergreens with scrambled egg on their branches.

On the contrary, at Chantilly the only permitted thing was nonchalance. Only the most impermanent and blossomy of tributes were allowed. Freesias, freesias everywhere in all the satin-cushion colours of lemon, violet and a dark rhubarb pink.

His brother-in-law, the sexual excédé, had organized it all for his fellow skaters at the Rink. For the last time he had taken them all on. Mim and Marie, two slender minarets in blowy black chiffon, the taller, heavier draped column that was Mme de Chassevent, the military silence of the colonel and, of course, his abject self. The Sioux had performed marvels of swish self-control, but he had shown them up all over the place by breaking down throughout the ceremony and blubbing with the chauffeurs.

Young Benoir had stared at him as if he had just crawled out of a sewer, but Castleton couldn't have cared less. He had no further use for young Benoir. All those omens, what a scream !

Mim had stood as far away from him as possible, and who could blame her, but the sexuel excédé had been a French brick about it all.

'Puss had it too rough. Don't wish him back, fella,' was what the French brick had said.

He was dead right. Because, whereas what had gone on before, up to, and including, the Rink had been awful, the actual being dead-and-buried-at-Chantilly part of it is all right.

It's very nice at Chantilly. He's with his father. In his rightful place. Where none of them, including himself, can get at him.

Especially himself. Castleton thinks : Poor dear. I must have bored him something shocking towards the end.

He has decided to scrap his Swissair connection at sixteen hours, partly because he has done nothing yet about freighting the Bentley back, but chiefly because he has noticed it is now well after eight o'clock.

He'll have to put a call through to London anyway, to let old Cecil know he's coming, though come to think, at this end of the week he'd be more likely to catch him at Ashwater. He may even call Tokyo and talk to the bank. Depends on a time check, of course, but if it's still during office hours over there it might be a good idea to get a first reaction to the probability of his taking over fairly immediately.

After that he'll have a bite of dinner somewhere in town, away from the hotel. He might even stay another night and catch an early flight. This latest plan has made him grin because by now, and knowing Benoir, his ex-brother-in-law will have tried to contact him in London at least twice. Well, he's on his own now, if he has ever been anything else, and he's in absolutely no hurry to get nowhere any faster than he must.

He feels suddenly better than he has felt for ages. The immediate need now is to get shot of the Pfitzer. A well-kept path leads him away from it, down a bosky dip and out by the tennis courts where couples are still playing by the sunset lake. Cries from the courts and from diving swallows mingle with noises from the distant town and from outlying meadows, where they're still getting in a second crop of hay, a dog's loud barking sounds very near.

Down on the lake a lit-up ferry is creeping almost imperceptibly to the other side where lights are already twinkling out along the lower slopes, and the faraway urgence of a chapel bell has just begun to sound.

A fine wandering rain that could be veils of midges or spray from sprinklers rotating on the lawns is fingering Castleton's face. He posts Benoir's letter still unopened down a grating and begins the last leg home. Above him, halfway up its private Alp, the vast hotel is lit up like an ocean liner.

Only the Ritz-Splendide to tackle now before he books his flight.

27

The Man from Pfitzerland

He can hear old Cecil's heart-warming bellow all over Main Arrivals. 'Here he is, bless him! Here's our chap!'

The Castletons are out in force to meet the man from Pfitzerland.

To*sher*! Hu*llo*!

Hu*llo*! Castleton shouts back. He's home and already thoughts of Wilton Place and Ashwater are putting him ten foot underground.

He finds himself kissing a shade too enthusiastically the large, fresh cheeks of his sister-in-law and those two strapping English Roses, his nieces Penny and Pam.

'Where are the Littles?' Castleton wants to know. The Littles are the younger half of Cecil's lot. Liddy, Samantha and Robin. He hasn't seen them since before Vol. I. He used to adore young Sammy. He isn't so sure about it now. Now he isn't sure about anything.

Old Cecil is telling him it would have been a bit much to get 'em up in time to meet his plane. They would have had to get up at eight bells or sparrow's fart or something, so darling Syb had thought it best to leave 'em at the Work'us.

The Work'us is the Castleton name for No. 38 Wilton Place. The Sioux aren't the only ones to have names for everything.

'They can't wait to see you, old darling.' Cecil adds fondly: 'They've got such shockin' colds, poor sweets. It'd break your heart to see their poor little red noses.'

'I shouldn't think so,' says Castleton callously.

They all walk out into the dark, warm August morning where oily brown leaves are lying about like stools in the dark pink light of dawn.

'Brekkies now,' chants old Cecil. He's as happy as a king lugging all the luggage and herding his lot towards the estate wagon which, amazingly, he has contrived to park fairly near an exit.

Old Cecil is persona grata with all officials, even the Heathrow police.

'Brekkies for babas.' He's as fatherly with his shower as Benoir is. Benoir had said of his riff-raff: 'I have washed my hands of that case.' By now, Castleton wouldn't mind betting, they're as thick as thieves again. Good for them, Castleton thinks, nothing could have been less right than his own assessment of that particular situation. All those omens. Come to think, he's been wrong about everything to do with the Sioux. Well, he's not going to start to rethink the whole thing now. Apart from being no use, his brain, for the time being, is not accepting any more messages.

It's August, but darling Syb is babbling on about Christmas at Ashwater, and the house-party she has planned for next week as ever is.

Sheena Sykes-Bladen is coming.

'You remember Sheena, don't you, Tosh? She's terrific value, old "Bill" Sykes. She's coming down for Christmas, too.'

The blessed girl is screaming at her young: 'Won't it be utter blissikins having darling old Tosh at Ashwater? I simply can't wait for Christmas!'

For a moment the air is darkened with cocktail shakers and desk sets in tooled leather, from Asprey's for Tosher with love.

This Christmas he was to have been initiated into tribal rituals of the Sioux and to have supped off legendary tablecloths that had cost human life. Now he has been condemned to four days of Ashwater, being chased by Bill Sykes.

'Oh, Mum! You've made Tosh go all mopey!' The girls plan to share a flat in Paris over Christmas with Trisha and Emma Cox-Dowding and an awfully nice American girl called Melanie Shimkus.

'Cripes,' says Castleton.

And cripes to him, too, say Pam and Penny. If it hadn't been for all this high drama they could have stayed in Paris with his stinking rich in-laws. 'We never had a chance to meet the Sioux. You are a bore, Tosh!' squeal Pam and Penny.

'I know.' It's a quite good description of him, actually. There had been a Frenchwoman behind him on the plane who had got him down very badly. An ersatz Mim. In the Customs he had made himself turn round and look at her, a fearsome and bedizened harpy who could not have looked less like Mim if she'd tried. But her clever perfume is still getting Castleton down.

Darling Syb is a handsome lass who stands, Castleton estimates, not less than five feet eight inches in her well-filled tights. Her arms are modelled on a figurehead's from Nelson's Navy and clank with bracelets, every seal on which is hefty enough to brain an ox. Her calves, forging ahead of Castleton like pistons, are hard and well-turned as the legs of a full-sized billiards table.

What does she *mean* by 'em? Castleton asks himself. He is unable to take his eyes off. He is incapable of being fair. He has now discovered that the hellish calves are dotted over with all sort of jolly moles, which are probably old Cecil's pride and joy but are no good at all to a Sioux addict like Castleton. He has only to look at them to know he is still in the worst of his withdrawal period.

They have arrived at the brake. 'Give 'em to me,' growls Castleton, snatching his grips from Cecil and hurling them in the boot. 'Bloody rupture yourself. Silly ass.' He gets in the back with Cecil and the girls.

There is the usual Castleton smell of bat oil and dog. The brake seems crammed with single Wellington boots as well as a beautiful Clumber spaniel bitch in heavy whelp.

Overfed brute. 'Get out,' snarls Castleton.

She gazes at him reproachfully with beautiful black-trimmed eyes and clambers heavily over the driving seat to subside, a softly groaning heap next to Syb. She's already leaking milk.

'Serves her right, silly bitch,' says Castleton, fanning the flames.

There are maidenly shrieks of 'Stinker!' and 'Do you *mind*?'

Cecil explains fondly: 'Poor old lady. Can't be left now. Too near her time.' He's mopping around the straddled legs with a duster.

Penny calls out: 'Do mind her, Daddy. Robin'll be livid if anything happens to her now. He's got a half-share in her litter and he's already spent the money.'

Young Robin doesn't know he's born yet, thinks Castleton sourly.

'He's done awfully well at his prep school, though,' offers Syb brightly, as if in answer to his thought. She has kicked off her shoes and is looking for her keys. The Clumber is slumped all over her as well as over the driving seat.

'She's a boofer-woofer!' she tells Castleton. 'She's so self-conscious about her tits. You'd have adored it last week, Tosh. We took her to the Pendle-Thing's dance.'

'Mum hoicked her on to Lady P's bed and she disgraced herself all over their rotten coats!'

'Their *scabby* tabbies!'

'Their *shabby* scabby tabbies!'

'Tosher is *not* amused!'

'Oops,' shriek Pam and Penny.

'She's a Woof-Boof!' declares Sybil, whom Castleton suspects of having quite a few variations on this theme. She has got rid of her hat by handing it over the back for Cecil to nurse. It is quite a nice hat, but it and Syb have never come to terms and are obviously still terrified of each other.

'I loathe titfers, don't I, Sissl? I only put one on for Tosh.' She smiles affectionately at her brother-in-law.

He smiles back. Her guileless forehead is marked by faint but ruler-straight lines acquired in Hong Kong.

She asks with fitting solemnity, 'How did you leave them all in Paris, Tosh?'

'I left 'em,' Castleton says.

'Eyes on the road, my poppet,' murmurs Cecil. She disregards the red light and runs happily on.

'Sissl says George was only ten.'

'Yup,' answers Castleton.

'Oh, Tosher, how too ghastly! Oh, isn't that too awful, Tosh!'

'Yup,' agrees Castleton cheerfully.

She careers onwards, jumping the lights.

'I expect you miss him *dreadfully*, don't you, Tosh? He was such a *happy* little fellow.'

'He was when he was dead,' says Castleton.

She stops for a moment then makes the bad mistake of driving on.

'He was such a *beautiful* child. I often said to Sissl, didn't I, Sissl? "George is such a *beautiful* child".'

'Yes, you did, darling,' murmurs Cecil quickly.

But Castleton says with the utmost brutality, 'They had to clean him up quite a bit before we recognized him.'

She stops.

Castleton explains blandly: 'We thought he'd never die.' That's shut her up. If she starts again, he'll let her have it again, till she finally belts up.

Under the hat he is gripping his brother's hand. He adores Old Cecil from the bright line left by his Admiralty bowler to the disarming mass of silky crushed curls at the back of his beautiful bonce.

Silly prick, thinks Castleton proudly, you're lovely.

He feels relaxed and comparatively happy, crushed

between Cecil and the girls, and only the light, dry perfume still bothers him much at all, while from the driving
seat darling Syb continues to dish out her deathless
rubbish. The nape of her neck is criss-crossed with lines
acquired in Malta.

'It's grand to be home,' declares the man from
Pfitzerland, who is nowhere near, and possibly never will
be, completely dried out.

A NOTE ON THE TYPE

This book was set on the Linotype in a type face called
Baskerville. The face is a facsimile reproduction of types
cast from molds made for John Baskerville (1706–1775) from
his designs. The punches for the revived Linotype Baskerville
were cut under the supervision of the English printer
George W. Jones. John Baskerville's original face was one
of the forerunners of the type style known to printers as
"modern face"—a "modern" of the period A.D. 1800.

Composed in Great Britain

Display typography composed by Maxwell Photographics, Inc.,
New York, New York

Printed and bound by The Haddon Craftsmen, Inc.,
Scranton, Pennsylvania

Display typography and binding design
by Marysarah Quinn